I0622302

Parallel Minds

Dee Lori's Table 42 -Evolution *Soul*ution series 1

Jolie DeMarco
Copyright 2012-2016

All rights reserved. This publication is designed to provide information in regard to the subject matter covered. It is sold with the understanding that the publisher is not engaged in rendering medical or other professional services. If medical, financial or other expert assistance is required, the services of a competent professional person should be sought. This book may not be copied or sold without legal permission from the author.

Parallel Minds
Dee Lori's Table 42

Okay, before I start- I want you to know- these are truly the names they used. I did not- I repeat did *not* make them up. You will see why later as we go on.

Nickname-Sonny the oddly cute female 28- writes restaurant reviews specifically for the consistency of food in South Florida for Frommerz Corporation. Frommerz is a humongous company that is a big deal job for her- I believe anyone for that matter.

It allows Sonny to eat free at the same restaurant once a week for 6 weeks in a row. This creative chic-constantly references and compares TV stars, models any famous person in her daily silly and sarcastic conversations. She's currently working on a book – called *My souls imprint- intriguing shorts*-in hopes of getting a sweet contract deal with Hay House publishing company.

Sonny constantly enters writing contests. The latest- is an entry with Createspace. She wants to win the $50,000 prize money. She's been manifesting this to happen.

Sonny feels it is her "purpose in life," -reaching as many people as she can through her writing. Aside from her writing aspirations she seriously expects to meet the man of her dreams sooner than later. Especially since she had a psychic that told her she would.

In the meantime - her girlfriend and sidekick -nicknamed Cher age 26 is also a writer, but for Blah magazine. It's Miami's hottest read. Cher gets paid to blog- world wide –on stuff that usually doesn't matter. She loves her job more than anything-

1

she lives to write and vice versa.

Cher 's faults slash gifts are one in the same .She likes to write *her* style- like she talks- and gets pissed when people correct her grammatically or on anything for that matter.

Cher has great success in her writings especially with Blah magazine but that doesn't seem to be enough. She comes up with many fruitful ideas on a daily basis and currently she wants to take action on each and every one of them. Some see Cher as an over thinking pain in the butt! She's a bit more narcissistic than Sonny. I feel she just wants to be heard. Cher is ecstatic that Blah Mag totally gets her writing style. Cher calls it "al la- me." Cher's translation- is *"my way."* She's has so many hats per say- she's really a bit off the wall at times.

Both Cher and Sonny are totally in a mindset that is causing them to want *more* in their lives. Both have nothing other than writing and talking about their work. The monotony of eating at the same order by number restaurant 6 weeks in a row – is causing havoc. It seems like their writing is defecating their brains from other excitements of life.

They actually make weekly bets of $60 bucks a pop! Who does that? I don't know whether to think they are incapable of normalcy or just lost. The bets they have are ridiculous and frankly, I feel like I am a little to blame for this behavior. It seems it could be looked as a grand gesture of what I do, but I seriously believe that it breaches the main purpose of what I stand for.

Their weekly $60 bet – actually has rules! They obviously made up this betting game. Each chick must have a total of 6 coffee dates-coordinating with their weekly paid by Frommerz dinner. No matter who has the coffee date both women attend the coffee house location. One of them just pretends they are chilling, sipping coffee- sitting alone. The other young lady is on the real date.

They meet these men online and from some new phone app that you can browse and look at pictures of guys and choose one to wink or hit on them… crazy chit.

Get this- they *both* try to read the man's aura! They read his energy patterns and/or use their telepathic abilities- which they *think* are good!

They both need an extreme amount of practice to be accurate. Sonny and Cher then meet after the coffee dates at the order by number restaurant to evaluate their findings of their men specimens! I don't know what the name of that restaurant– I forget the name they told me .I just know it's got a lot of pasta options to order on the menu.

I'm going to go back to their literal conversations because this will help you understand what I am trying to express.

Cher says to Sonny: You- are *so* abnormal!
Every time we come to *your* restaurant pick- I have to listen to *your* short stories. What about me! *Me*, ME!

On top of that- I am a bit jealous since *you* get paid to eat and write about food on Frommerz's dime. The fact that you get to take me is *your* bonus.

Can you see I'm pointing at my face and I'm smiling big? Now-*You* have to listen to my new creations of writing. My fabulous magazine articles and trash the public loves to read- just for Blahhhhhhhhhhhhhhhh. I'm a genius.
I love my freaking job. They let me write whatever I want and the way I want.

Sonny says: Yes. I know *you* love to write like you talk. You say that over and over. You really gloat-and ya know half of what you say and write –it's not always proper English or grammar!
You are damn straight, that you are one lucky *bitach* they *allow*

3

you to have that job!

Wow we are really being sarcastic asses tonight to each other. Let me re-phrase that. We are extremely acting unconsiderate towards each other this evening.

Cher: You mean-In- inconsiderate. You are such a moron!

Sonny: Whateva. After we order, I'm going to read first okay?

Cher: Yes master… you can read yours first.   What are you going to order?

Sonny: I'm going to get my own creation! See it says here on the menu- you can order by number or create your own mess—I mean dish.
Muoohaaaa-hahha. I create. I make dinner good. Me wants Fusilli…yummm.
Then I want fresh tomatoes. I want black olives, fresh basil, fresh oregano and a touch of anchovy paste. I'm going to eat better than Mirah Carey on her birthday.

Cher: Okay. Here we go. Don't embarrass me. This is the first time we are eating here and have 5 more times. *We* –have to eat here. Don't embarrass me with your "*me – I* -talk".
It's funny but please refrain when the new hottie waiter comes to take our order. Look- we got that cute young guy. Remember - never tell him our names.

Sonny: Yeah I know. We are incognito. You are *a known* critic -at least *you* think you are!

Cher: Ahh, he lookie good. Okay. Shut up. Here he comes. Be normal.

Waiter: Hi ladies, hope you are having a good evening. Can I get you some drinks? Are you ready to order?

Sonny: This is our first time. I'm meant our first time here.

Waiter: My name is Dev. Our concept is that we have 41 pasta dishes on the menu; each explains what ingredients are in each one listed. Or you can choose from the types of pasta and add any hot or cold toppings you like. You can use them with any variation of the pasta sauces. Each dish is twenty bucks-

Cher: I like that. Neat concept. I would like an iced tea and I need a few minutes… she knows what she wants

Sonny: Hi, yes I want water with lemon, hot water please. Then I want to build my own dish. I am going to do the fusilli with fresh tomatoes, black olives; capers, a fried egg, fresh basil, fresh oregano and a touch of garlic add some olive oil and a small amount of marinara.

Cher: Dev, what would you suggest? What is the best dish here? What one is your favorite?

Dev: Well, this always makes me uncomfortable when people ask me. Only because there are so many great ones. I've   truly tired all 41 dishes as is- and I like number 18 and 11.
But I find it best for people to pick their own. Plus they can't get pissed at me!
  Like #11 is spicy and hot-
#18 is good if you like sausage. This one is sweet with a lot of garlic.

Sonny: She likes *all* of that. Yep. All of it.
 Cher: Ya know- I will just have the same creations she made. Thank you for your input.

 Dev: Okay you got it. I'll put the order in and bring out your drinks. Thank you.

Cher: *Why,* Sonny? Why do you always have to do that! He's gonna think we are psychos *and* like him. We have to come back

5 more times- he's gonna put the freak alert on us!
Just be half normal okay?
Damn you. I love and hate you all at the same time.
Now, I will torture you with my creative mind....

Sonny: Haa..Heehaw I'm so cute. Begin. Read on- my dear gal.
Read on.

Cher: Okay...eh hem. My souls imprint a book of intriguing
shorts. Here's Number one:

Dev: Here are your drinks. Your dinners will be ready in about
15 minutes. The owner does each dish fresh. If you need me just
yell.

Cher and Sonny: Thank you.

Sonny: I know under your breath Cher- you thought "thank you
hottie- and that he looks like a young Brad Pitt.

Cher: I'm ignoring you. I am reading my short now. Here's my
opening line to the book:

"A soul's imprint is person's experiences and moments. The soul
is simply the energy that holds and collects these occurrences
and can save them or let go of them depending on the person's
intention.

Intention is what you desire and project.

All in all-each scenario, life situation, dream, parallel-past life -
whatever label you want to give it- tells the experiences of your
life within it- *in energy form.*
Everything is energy. Your voice and your thoughts.

Here are some of my most interesting soul imprints..."

Sonny: This is my first short story in the book- I did some
minor research on some paranormal stuff- So some of this is

6

winged. I'm not sure if I used the best way of verbalizing the characters. Judge me lightly. It's a work in progress.

Cher: I know! Just read it already.

Sonny: Okay...here it goes.

A friend once told me, that people- in general have an attention span of 8 seconds.

Every year it becomes less and less according to experts.

Cher: Wait. Is that even a true fact?

Sonny: Don't interrupt me. I told you its rough draft!

In the future it will certainly be less due to the label called Attention Deficits Disorder. Many understand this label to be caused by environmental toxins.

I wrote these *short* stories to enlighten your minds.

Soul Short *numbah* 1

"Are you thinking about when you experienced wonderful things in life? Like being age 22 and free? Or when you drove your red jeep wrangler to South beach? The trip to Miami with 3 friends in the back seat singing lady Gaga's hit song. "I was born this way."

What about when your drove back home to New Jersey from college in Florida? You drank 6 cups of coffee at the rest stop and ended up back in Florida when you were previously in South Carolina!

You *still s*wear someone switched the freeway sign.

What about when you met Brett Favre and had no idea who he was?

I know ... what about when you turned 30 and you had the best year ever- you opened a flower shop and dated some really great guys.

Ohhh. Oh, the best was when you went for that job interview and specifically wore the color green because you thought *the man* hiring you loved money- you were right, Donald Trump did hire you!

What about *how I noticed you* and *you noticed me* in the gluten free aisle in the grocery store.
It was a long familiar look- since we had seen each other many times around town previously. I remember you said "Hello" to me when I was having a difficult day and I instantly felt better.

By the way, this is me- Kara Brady. I am talking to you telepathically. I know you are upset and trying to decide to cry or call 911- because you just found me on the supermarket floor.

Thank you for listening… as I think of my beautiful life memories. I can see them clearly. Please know you *ARE* hearing me- you *aren't* crazy.

I really had a great life- I have the best mother, father and sister.

The end.

Cher: OMG! That freaking gave me chills up my spine, arms and legs! That one is crazy! I love it! You will win an award with work like that. I'm jealous that was brilliant!
Imagine if you just read that- and I didn't know it was a story. Powerful stuff. Did you copyright it yet?

Sonny: Yes! You know I always copyright everything! You loved it? Me too. I actually think this is one of my best creations. I have a few more. I wrote this one last Friday. Some of my shorts were inspired by dreams. I've been dreaming really a lot lately and remembering stuff to write.

8

Cher: Read another one. This place is taking forever to bring out our food.

Read on- it kills some time till our foods out.

Sonny: Okay. Here's my one point fiver. A super mini short.

Soul Short #1 point Five.

I call it- one to ponder.

Did you ever think dying at 51 years old would be acceptable? Because if you could accept dying at age 51, it would seem old enough-But what if- in reality- you were going to die at age 48? Kind of like a trick to catch you off your guard- so then- you would not expect it- and there would be no fear or worries around death?

Some people believe once you pass- you can contact other people telepathically that are currently alive- mind to mind connections."

Sonny: I'll just read one more. Oh hold -up, here comes the waiter…

Dev: Hi, sorry ladies, the dinners are taking longer than expected. The chef makes all the pasta fresh and is out of fusilli. Do want different kind of pasta? He's making more now. We just have been super busy with season here in Florida, you know. Right?

Cher: We know. It's not your fault. We can wait- if you get us our drinks. We girls like to chat anyway.

Dev: Okay thanks for being cool about it. It's still going to be about another 15-to 20 minutes. I'll bring your drinks asap.

Sonny: No prob.

Sonny: Okay. Lucky *you*- Cher. You get to hear one more short!

Cher: I'm ready.

9

Sonny: My soul short number deaux. I call it "FIVE YEARS FORWARD-33 THIRTY THREE" I might change that. I dunno yet. Okay here it goes:

There is bunch of people here at the lake today.

I talk to myself quite a lot these days.

My thoughts are vivid and sometimes tiresome. I realized when I had written my thoughts I *can* let them go.

Today I am at the lake its December 1st and I live in Florida.

I could have gone to the beach, but decided I wanted to be around less people- at least today that is how I feel.

I'm sitting alone -people watching- one of my favorite things to do. I see groups of kids, families and teeny boppers - havin their kicks in the water. I think I will get my ass in the water too, its 86 degrees today. I'm sweating and look like crap.

Lucky me I can go in the water in December to cool off. Yes, that was *sarcasm* to myself. The best part about writing a journal is that no-one fu*king corrects me on my grammar. I hate that shit- nobody talks like a novel anymore. We tweet –we short cut *everything*- we are the epiphany of less and always want more. Did I spell that correctly? A- pit-ame sound right...Ughhh.

I tried to write a book with someone once- and all they did was correct me-grammatically. Loved my ideas but I felt like the judge was gonna cut off my head if I didn't get every punctuation perfect. That didn't work out. As long as you can understand what I am saying what's the big deal on that. Okay, self- let it go...

I'm going in the water...

I'm back writing again. I was just in the lake and hung out- it felt like 2 minutes- I put my whole body including my head under the water to cool off. When I came up out of the water the whole lake cleared out. It was like there was a fire alarm and all the people left. Weird. I actually feel weird too. Like an off balance kind of feeling.

 There was groups of people now I see only 1, 2 ,3 4, 5, 6, 7 Ahhh 8 people- that includes me…
 What the heck- did I pass out or something?
I'm now sitting near my set up, my umbrella, towel- my stuff is all here. Or if I wrote it properly it would be "sitting by my belongings,"-my notebook obviously and my towel and chair are here- I'm looking around and it looks like a lot of chairs and towels are still here without people...

Maybe I'm having one of those dreams where I astral travel. Ya know people like me do that, we meditate, we do yoga, and we do energy healing... all that psychic shizzle.

I've done that – astral travel-not on purpose but when I fall asleep sometimes I travel or do a cross over. That's lingo the peeps I hang out with. We call it- "mindful lingo" or crunchy granola living style- Ahhh whatever why am I explaining this to myself?"

Sonny: This is where I need to get more info – I want to do some research for this part .Go into what astral travel is and a crossing over in details. I don't know anything about it as of now – so I need to get on that!

Cher: Awe- Come on. Read it. It was just getting good. Keep going. What else you got so far?

Sonny: Okay. But it's not perfect yet. Yet. I stress on that!

"The 7 others that are still here at the lake…they are a very different bunch of people. They all seem to look lost and out of it.
 I am going to talk to this boy- he looks like a mini Brad Pitt. He

11

said he was 12 but looked like he was 16 or 17. He had a very immature demeanor.

Cher: Hahahha. See- you say everyone looks like Brad Pitt or someone. I love the stupidity of it! Continue. Please.

Sonny: Don't interrupt. I am reading.

I asked mini Brad – his name. He said it's actually Brett. He says he was here with his family and they just disappeared. Brett didn't see them leave, but they were gone. He feels a bit dazed. His words descriptions of how he is currently feeling seemed hazy.

I saw two girls that are sisters. One is crying she's about 11. And the other girl looks like she's 16. I'm going to talk to them too.

Sonny: I scribbled some notes here that's why I am hesitating to read further-(Note*both older looking than she really is- than 5 years forward hint here- since none of the kids can see themselves -no mirrors they don't realize it either.)

Both girls are actually 11. They are twins. I knew they were sisters as they don't look exactly alike but have similar features. Both have a pointy nose that fits their features beautifully. They are such cute girls, Kelly and Katherine.

The same thing happened to them they were in the water and poof- parents gone. They were up in the grassy area. They were gone when the girls swam up and out of the water. They were swimming and racing each other beforehand.

I decided this was way too weird all of these kids-except me. I called out to all 7 that were there - "all of you – please come here- can I ask you something?" this is what I yelled to them all.

All 7 of the teens came closer to me.

I asked them," who did you come with? And are they gone?" - It was the same scenarios that I noted with the twins and Brett.

There was Stevie age 15, Karen 12, Terrance 14, Vashita 11, the twins were both 11, Brett age 7 and me age 33. I thought – kids- these days *really* look older than there real age. It *must* be the hormones in the fast food.

All of us were in the water fully when this happened. Whatever - *this* is.

Our heads and bodies were under the lake water.

As of now-
We can't see anything around us except the lake and the grassy area that was there previously; no people just 8 of us.
No birds, no flies-nothing. It's almost too quiet.

We decided to wait to see if any of the parents come back. Since I am the oldest I feel like the mother here- and I can't just leave them.

I started to look around a bit and noticed that my car wasn't there either. There was nothing around us. Just the lake and grass as far as all of us could see.

Now I was getting scared but didn't want to spook the kids.

I suggested we all hang together and wait to see if anyone would come back.

At this point I am really starting to freak out!

I am holding in my emotions – but something is *really not good* here.

I started a circle – I had all the kids sit in a circle and tell me a little about themselves. I did this to keep them occupied. We talked a lot about where and when we were born. Since I know a lot about astrology I told them their zodiac signs. As we

13

continued to talk- all of them including me are Scorpios! All of us born between Oct 26- November 22. This really freaked me out.

I started thinking of all the cosmic occurrences that were coming or just recently past. I remembered that the suns rotation around the earth and would do a polar flip. This happens every 11 years. And we just had an asteroid miss the earth's atmosphere…

I didn't want to scare anyone so I just kept writing in my journal as the kids played some games in the lake.

Brett the 12 year old screamed bloody murder from the center of the lake… Scared the shit out of all of us and I   thought maybe he hit his head on a rock or something.
I flew into the water and grabbed him. He was synged from something in the lake. It was hot; it was like his skin was burnt on a hot iron.

I swam Brett out of the water and to the grass. Luckily I had coco nut oil in my bag- I put it over his burns as he yelped in pain. Everyone was out of the lake -the moment he screeched in angst. I asked if everyone else was okay.
I heard:

Yes. Yes. Yes. Yes. Yes. Yes I am had gotten all kids confirmed that they were fine.
Come here. Let's all stay close.

I asked Brett if he saw anything- he said he felt metal or something big and hard in the water – he didn't realize it was hot till he grasped it with his hand and his leg had touched it.

I asked if anyone had eye goggles –I wanted to go in the water- I had to see what this was- I was scared as shit. I walked slowly towards the middle of the lake. Then once I couldn't reach the bottom- I went under and swam into the center area place where Brett got hurt.

A huge f*cking metal boulder! It had a satellite receptor on it. It looked like it came from NASA or outer space. It was still hot. I could feel the water as I got closer to it. It felt like it was 20 degrees hotter. It must have been over 110 degrees in the water- the metal must be close to 200 degrees for it to singe Brett's skin.

As I got closer, I decided it was too hot and I got out of the water. When I reached the grass, each of the kids asked me "what ya see? What is it? Is it a monster? Is there a plane in there?"

No- no... NO! I screamed! I couldn't hold in my fear. Then I realized I freaked them all out- so I pulled my fear inside and said its fine... We are all going to be fine.

This is a sign… it's just a big piece of metal that fell or something. I tried to talk like I knew what was happening, but had no freaking clue.

Okay everyone, let's create a circle again- let's see what else we have in common. I want to write about each one of you in my journal- I grabbed my notebook.

I said to all the kids: this is important that we all share and talk- I will write everything I can about each of you and we will find out what is going on this way… I was really just trying to calm myself and them at the same time. We started one by one.
Name birth, parents, siblings, where they were born and what's the favorite food and color- the school they attended and so forth.
I started with Terrance.
He said he was in grade school- that didn't make sense. I didn't want to challenge him, but I said "Terrance, you said you are 14 years old, right? Then how could you be in 7th grade?
He answered me. "I am 14. I am I swear. I am not a liar... "

I quickly said, "No. I didn't mean that, I guess I'm too old to know what grade is what... Sorry..." and I apologized to him.

Next was Karen she was 12- but said she was in 5th grade? How can that be?
I know I am no expert in schools but this made no sense. The twins said: "yeah that's not right- if you are 12 you would be in 7th grade!

Each kid told me their age and the school level – nothing matched. Each kid was 5 years off- which calculated to five years ahead of what they said.

Brett said in a funny voice – "well, I do feel taller today." Then the twins said: "Me too- and bigger", Vashita said her clothes fit so much tighter than earlier today.
I feel like this is a scene in a movie.

This can't be happening... Hey Brett... Come here can you punch me? "What? "He said. I can't. That is not nice. My mom said never hit a girl.

Well Brett today is different. I asked you to- so you won't get in trouble. I promise.

Go ahead right here, hit me on my face- just a slap okay. Okay. I don't want to hurt you.
You won't- just a slap... Please...
Brett slaps me in the face. I feel it alright. Thanks kid.

Are you okay? He asked. Yes, I'm fine thank you.
I told Brett he did a good job.
Why did you want me to do that he asked.

I said I just needed to wake up. I told him I was feeling sleepy.

That confirms it. I am awake *and* this is happening.

It felt like it had been 8 hours, but I looked at my cell phone-and dammit- it's not working!

We have no idea what time it is.

Terrance yelled super loud to me- "hey we can tell by the sun. I took a Boy Scout class and we can tell by the sun."
   All eight of us looked up in sync and just saw clouds. Dammit I said.

Crap!
Maybe later it will clear up and we can see what time it is.
Terrance yelled. Does anyone have a watch?

Katie yelled I do. Let me see- I saw her disappointed face as she told me her watch had also stopped .She said" I wasn't supposed to wear it in the water- that what mom said."

I said its okay honey, it will be okay. It might just need another battery- don't get upset. We are all fine.

I decided to use another approach- me myself and I. None of the kids knew this and I didn't share it. But I am a psychic for a living. Since it seemed we are out of options. I had to assume we were stuck in some sort of vortex or parallel dimension. What else could it freaking be?

If it was just me I would just say I went mad, kookoo like my great aunts- but I'm with 7 children I don't know well and it's real!

I decided to try to channel spirits. I was going to try to connect telepathically with my friend Elaine to see if she could hear me telepathically. Mind to mind.

We did lots of practices on telepathy and I actually formed a telepathic team for fun.

I sat off to the side of the children and tried to meditate. I asked them all to keep quiet and try to take a nap- then I would wake them later.

Some of them went to sleep. Others couldn't and just stared out to the sky.

I projected my message and directed to Elaine. I projected this message:" I am stuck at the lake area on 3rd street in the lake park Florida. I am with 7 others- please help. "

After what felt like 20 minutes- I heard- telepathically "hey I hear you-

It was Elaine. I sensed her energy.

"I asked her to come to the lake area. She replied "I will be there in 30 minutes. See you then."

I waited and waited. It felt like eternity. I heard "I'm here." It sounded like Elaine's voice. I looked around the lake area and replied: "No you are not. I cannot see you."

Elaine replied:" I have my feet in the lake." I'm looking at the tree on the north part of the lake."

I am here-. I am."

I started to cry. I knew she could not see me- or I her.

We – the kids and I-were not where Elaine was. I know she knew the location of the park because we would usually go there - I mean *here* together occasionally.

This leads me to believe *we* are on another parallel.

I asked Elaine to find out some info– I asked to call around and see if something did happen here? At the lake. I used mental abilities and again ,telepathically said to her "We are here – I found a metal space thing in the lake. Help pleaseeee."

I heard Elaine say she would I will call police-and she will help." "Stay where you are", she mind talked to me.

Elaine went to the police. They had some missing kids reported but Elaine didn't have any info to give the police- such as names - so the police couldn't help her without them.

She looked in the newspapers to see if there was something that fell from the earth or anything weird. Nothing was reported.
Finally she called the FBI. They took her in and said they *did* do some experimenting in that lake.
They told her that the FBI had a component- it was made to send vibrations to the space module in northern Florida. They did transmit this on December 1, 2013. She told them everything she could. They told her she could not tell anyone or contact the news.
They wanted to keep it hidden. Since they knew there had been missing persons.

Elaine telepathically communicated as much as she could- the message I received was broken.

I heard parts, but I knew that no one would come help. We had to try something else.

Elaine said something about being Dec 3rd- that was only 2 days later than when I wrote in my journal. Well it was currently today- to us.

We sat as a group- all 7 kids and myself. We talked about a variety of subjects and then, the question came. "Are we being taken by aliens? Are we captured?"

"Will they take our brains..? Were we drugged?"
I finally told them what I knew -and what I thought was going on. They all looked at me like I was teaching them something they were interested in.

I felt horrible because I was hoping it wasn't true. That we would all wake up and walk out of a movie theatre.

I said to the kids "There's been a fast forward in time. Each one of us was under the water- a government experiment was done with that metal satellite. It created vibrations that accelerated time.

It took us as of now 2 days in the future. But all of you are 5 years ahead. This I can't understand.

Maybe you aged 5 years faster in 2 days. I am not sure. Maybe I did too. I can't see me to tell you.

I know I am here to help all of you. I don't know how, but I will try to figure it out. I am trying to contact as many people as I can. Like I explained to you earlier- I am telepathic and can talk with vibrations to other people. I can try to contact your parents or whomever you want for you – I don't know if they will hear me- but I can try.
I can tell you that all of us are Scorpios and we are strong. There was a movement in the cosmos that affected the moon in Scorpio which means we –all of us here were in the water which makes vibrations easier to move faster and the same time the earth moved to a polar opposite.

I know some of you have no clue what I am saying... I'm sorry I don't know how to explain this to you in terms you can understand.
I just can say it as I know. Forgive me."

They looked at me clueless and some of them were upset.

I started to talk aloud- not knowing if they were really listening or understood. I just needed to express my thoughts out loud.
I said "In numerology, let me go back... Scorpios are usually insightful and feel emotions, and many have psychic abilities. This means you can connect with vibrations. This is how I "spoke "with my friend Elaine.
I can try to teach you to talk mind to mind with vibrations and we as a group can try to reach our friends family to help us or

talk to us." I explained it was similar to cell phone, we cannot see the connection with our eyes but the vibrations and frequencies can connect for contact.

Back to talking inside my head, I thought- Okay I have an idea... as I become desperate for wanting relief of being the leader for the children- I decide to *attempt* to be a walk-in . I will try to walk into another person to be on that parallel dimension and get us help.

I sat in silence and projected my mind and energy to go into another host body on Dec 1, 2013 the day we believe we are at the lake and are missing.

   Boom-I felt like I was in a body. It was a female about the same age- I was able to connect and ask the soul of that person to step aside just for us to receive help. The soul agreed. I thanked the soul and began – it was actually the same day December 1, 2013! I was in a woman's body -on that other dimension we were previously living before the government experiment.
I knew I could do something to stop the event *or* let the proper authorities know what might happen. The body I was in then drove to the lake – she the host body, went there early that day and told everyone to leave.
When the host body I was within was at the location of the lake, through *her* eyes- I saw my body – literally saw myself there. I was sitting in my chair , biting my lower lip and writing in my journal.

 For some reason the body I was in wouldn't walk up to me at the lake- I knew I was supposed to leave. I saw everyone going out of the water and getting into their cars- everyone left. The body I walked into - the host body also left the lake. The mission was complete.

I felt really awkward. I felt strange for a few minutes and then I came back into my body.

I looked around and all the children were nowhere in sight. I was still at the lake. I was in the water. I felt confused and tired. I walked up to the grass to lay down. I wasn't sure if I should be relived or upset. All the kids were gone. I hoped they were safe. I picked up my cell phone- it was on- it was working!! I cried hysterically! Its 1:11!

In numerology the number 1 means take time to breathe- relax and #11 means making a choice right from wrong. Decide on a positive or negative- and to make that decision now!

I closed my eyes – I squeezed them hard and decided to open them again quickly.

I looked around me and I was in Elaine's treatment room. I looked around the serene blue room - I realized I awoke out of a reiki energy healing session- whereas I reached one of my parallel lives.

Elaine counted backwards from 8, 7, and 6, 5, 4, 3, 2, 1 and stated: "This concludes our session-then she looked at me laying on the massage table and said:" You chose *this* one." and she quietly laughed. I was so glad I wasn't in that *other* place!

The weirdest part about this whole story is ----------------that I saw this whole short story in a dream on December 1st.

Then on December 3rd, 2 days later. That night at 10 pm- I had the television on while I was writing. I heard the TV NEWS station report- "there was a cosmic event today NASA in Florida launched a --- blah blah blah and it was in the air –it was 33 minutes after it was in the air. People spotted it and thought it was an alien aircraft- people reported and posted about this siting on social media."

Sonny: Okay that's the end. Do you like it? I know it was long? Was it confusing?
Cher: I love it too; I don't know which short I liked better. But

this one is incredible too. Wow, the detail was amazing in the writing. I felt like I was there with the character and all those kids. It seemed so real. It really grabbed me.

Sonny: Well I don't want to show you the notes, cause I didn't fix all the grammar and the punctuations and all that.
Cher: You know it doesn't matter, because when you read it to me I felt it. I *felt* the fear- the *wonder*- it was all melting together and it got me. I got it all. And I really wanted more of it. You should think about making that one longer. I could see it as a full book.
Sonny: Really?
Cher: Yes. Absolutely.

Sonny: Dinner! Yeah! I'm starved.
Cher: Me too! This food better be out of this world for the wait!
Dev: Hi ladies, thanks again for waiting. Your pasta combo looks really good. Let me know if you need anything? Do you want some parmesan cheese?
Cher: No, I'm good thanks.
Sonny: Me too. No cheese. Thanks.

Cher: This is really good. I love the flavors. Great choice.
Sonny: Sure- I could eat this 6 times! Hahahha
Cher: Yeahas, because *now* I have to!

After dinner that night they were hanging out at a wine bar and a yoga teacher told Cher about a local spiritual publication. The yogi told her it had listings of several new age places that might help her with her research for the book she was writing.

The bar was crowded and Cher and Sonny noticed that all the men there were quite pigs. They watched this one man hit on a drunken lady.

Cher: He's a real piece of work. I can't believe he would hit on

her knowing she's annihilated.
Sonny: That's lack of morals right there.

Cher: At least her friends are telling him to get lost.
Sonny: Yeah. Good thing or I would've.
Cher: Let's go, there just creeps here. We will never meet a nice guy in a bar anyway.
Sonny: Yes. I know. Let's just go home. I'm done.

The ladies went home and watched the Television series the 4400. It was a show of a human race that had been taken into the light- there were 4400 people that were missing from the year 1945 till the present day. The show was super cool to them because it was all things they were currently interested writing about. Telepathy, psychic powers- it was inviting them to open their imagination. They watched 3 episodes on Netflix and called it a night. Sonny lived a few blocks away - she had her car that night, she drove home around 11pm.

Dinner Number Two Dos

That next week on Thursday at 6pm was the second night they ate at the same restaurant. This was where both ladies would talk and express themselves. They would talk about their week. Sonny had a lot of articles to write for her bog job and Cher needed to write a feature piece for Blah magazine by Monday afternoon.

Cher has some crazy tips on who to talk to for an interview with the singer Pink! She was going to be in town for her new album and Cher was trying to catch her to talk about her new movie part. It was going to be a feature because Pink was doing a movie and that was not something she normally does as a singer. Cher wanted to be the one to ask Pink if she liked acting better than singing. Although, we are all sure *we* know that answer. Last September Blah mag reported her as the best singer of all

24

time and wanted to give her a party in south beach- but nothing ever came of it. I guess her agent didn't want her in the crazy Miami scene- who knows.

On this particular Thursday, Cher unknowingly had another brilliant idea according to Sonny. Here's exactly how it went:

Sonny: Same table as last week, maybe the hostess will *always* sit us in the far corner.

Cher: They will. Especially when they hear *your* disturbing cackle laugh. You sound like a pig and an elephant doing it. They won't want all their customers thinking that lady from the TV series FRIENDS is dating what's his name again?
You know- the nerdy one that Monica ended-up dating- the Chandler dude! That's it. Remember he dated that woman with the black hair and she snorted and sounded like an animal while she was laughing. She had that annoying voice they all hated?

Sonny: Yes. I remember- Chandler kept on dating her and he also hated her voice. I guess. I really gave you a nice compliment on your laugh. Is his name it Chandler or Channeller? Chandelier—sounds French when I say it with an accent.

Cher: Look the same waitron man is coming to help us.

Sonny: Sweet. I do likie him . Dev was his name. Right?
Cher: Yes. Like you really didn't remember. Nice try. very smooth of you- I know you have a supermega crush on him, don't play me sista.

Sonny: You are so white bread.

Dev: Hey ladies- oh hey- you were here before. Last week sometime- I guess you liked the food.
Cher: Yep the food. We liked it a lot. Yep- a lot. My new favorite place.

Dev: Well good. What can I get you to drink tonight? Want a wine? We have a special tonight on red house. Only $6 a glass.

Sonny: Okay bring us each one- and we both are having the fusilli with fresh tomatoes, black olives; capers, a fried egg, fresh basil, fresh oregano and a touch of garlic add some olive oil and a small amount of marinara.

Dev: Got it. I remember now- the fried egg thing threw me off last time, kinda strange combo. I guess it was good since you are getting it again. Both the same. Okay. I'll be back with the wines.

Cher: Thanks Dev.

Cher: You are so hot for him- he's like 17. You are a cougar.
Sonny: No. Cougars are in their 4os.

Cher: Not uahh, it's just when your batting outside you age category.

Sonny: Who told you that? Nice analogy though…

Cher: I hope are food comes on time. Hey I wanted to show you this spiritual magazine, it's mostly ads but remember the research you wanted to do on astral travel stuff for your short story? Cause you said you were clueless- this might have some place to get info. Ya know all that whacky. ..kooky .. stuff.

Look at this ad of this lady- she teaches all kinds of stuff. She's a psychic and a teacher. I looked her website up earlier and she's done lots of cool things. She wrote books too. You'd be impressed... I was.

Sonny: Anyone impresses you- does she look like a

Cher: She looks pretty normal! I thought you would want to meet her because she wrote books on parallels and telepathic stuff.

I thought she would be a good person to check out. Since she looks okay. Cause her website pictures were nice'n normal. Not like some of those *other* ads. They were a bit over the top – they had ladies with tons of gold jewelry- like 50 rings on their fingers! Nor did this psychic lady I like -have witch black painted fingernails-I could see they were not painted or neutral.

Let me tell you -there were quite a few scary ones in the ads! Some of them were Wicca. Their advertisement said it! Right in their advertisement –think-about-it, Wicca-that means a *real* witch-

Who needs one of those? Maybe I'm just missing something?

Sonny: Wicca is cool now. It just means they practice witchcraft or ceremonies. It doesn't mean they are bad per say- but I guess black finger nails would sway me to think otherwise. So what did *this* psychic look like …? I mean it seems you did a whole background check. Her finger nails were neutral?
You are such a weirdo.
Who looks at that?

Cher: You will thank me someday for my details!
She looks like she could've worked at Hooters years ago, but now she is old.

Sonny: Please- don't say that if we go there to meet her! Please.

Cher: I wouldn't do that. But she looks like that lady similar to – dang. I don't know who, she looks like a lady-chick that we'd see around town.

Sonny: Look, it says right here. That there is a class tonight at 8pm." Learn how to read energy and auras" and next week same time "how to manifest what you want." Let's go after dinner! Wanna?

Sonny: Your nuts. You really want to go? If you do, I will go *with* you.

Cher: With me? This is for *your* research!

Sonny: Yeah sure- and I'm the Queen of England- you mean for your curiosity!

Cher: Speaking of Queens... I bet you $60 bucks that our waiter thinks we are dikes.

Sonny: What? Why do you think Dev thinks that?

Cher: It's our second time here... *Together,* and *you* ordered for both of us!

Sonny: Oh. Maybe. Whatever! He's 17 who cares- what he thinks! Besides, you...of course.

Cher: We don't know he's 17. He could be 28 and just has babyish face like Aston Kutcher.

Sonny: Here we go! I know you want me to ask him!

Cher: Speaking or relationships- *we have none.*
Sonny: I know-
Cher: I'll bet you sixty bucks that I will have a date for this weekend.
Sonny: What good does that do me?
Cher: True dat.
Sonny: Foods here.

Cher: Did I tell you I bet my boss yesterday? I bet him 50 dollars that I would get my game show -I'm writing -on Television. Not just web TV but Real TV!
Sonny: You're an ass- your boss must think you have a

gambling problem. And that you're an ass.
Cher: Just eat your food Bitach!

Both girls have such sarcastic tongues. When I first talked to them I figured that was the norm of their age. But now I see that they are really funny, and just are silly.

Sonny: You never told me the concept of the TV show. What is about?
Cher: Okay but this is top secret- if you tell anyone especially Lindsay Lohan she will sell the idea for drugs and then some dumb ass nobody will be the show host.

Sonny: Oh your thoughts my dear. Surely are *never* reality... Please do go on and share.

Cher: This is major- It is a game show. There is a real Judge – I would want a woman judge. There are 3 psychics on the panel for judging by using their special intuitive abilities. The guest is always just a regular joe shmo person. The regular person is taped before and after the show.

First the Joe gets taped talking about if they are selling a lie to the judge. It can be for example a lie or truth- That's the name of the game show. LIE OR TRUTH!
The Joe then comes out into the live audience with the judge and the 3 psychic panelists. Joe tells the lie or truth to the judge- Only one lie or truth. Basically, a fake'o story -or true facts.

Then- the psychics use their powers to judge the Joe and state if Joe is lying or telling the truth about their statement to the judge. The judge also makes a call if the JoeSmo is telling the truth or not. Then the tape is revealed – the Joe's previous recorded confession on video tape truth or lie is seen by the audience and all the judges.

Whoever is most accurate in the judgment, receives money. Do *ya* get it?

There's more.... In the meantime, the audience and all the peeps at home watching on TV can text in their votes, not only for truth or lie, but for their fav psychic or the judge to get it correct. Don't answer that yet-

Sonny: Too bad people can't place bets on this game show- or maybe they will be able to- *in Vegas*... Hmmm.
Cher: Let's keep it legal.

Cher: Wait... There's even more!
So now that the audience can see who is accurate in the panel of psychics, over the whole season, the psychics or the judge have chances to make a big score of money on the outcome of the Joes that are telling the truth or lying! This causes a frenzy of advertisers endorsing the psychics and all that! Plus the monies from the texting will go towards the person that wrote the show... That's called alaaaaaaaaaaaaaME!

Sonny: I think we need to call Simon Cowell- calling all money men-Ring.Rrrr.. Ring—answer the cell phone Randy Jackson!

Cher: What about J – lo, she's an intelligent woman. She's all into making the coin. She's works it with merchandise, videos, movies, clothing. She knows it all.

Sonny: Yeah I like her.

Cher: I'm ready. I copyrighted the show idea.

Sonny: Yeah, you totally have to do that. I had a friend that worked as an extra, she shared her TV show idea, and BAM it was on next season and the chick she told owning her idea. That Bitach! Nothing she could do!

Sonny: What show was it?

Cher: It was the idea of Hugh Hefner- you know that old show with the 3 Playboy chicks wanting to be in the magazine – they lived in the old dudes house and were *his* girl toys and finally he let them be in the magazine.

Sonny: OH. Dumb show- but I'm sure it made millions. That rat bastard stealin'ideas…

Cher: I know – why can't people come up with their own shit! Stealing creativity is just a dirt move.

Sonny: Hey- hurry up and finish eating. If you want to make that psychic class- we gotta fly.

Cher: Okay. Let's get Dev for the check.
Sonny: Before we go I want to give a prediction of when I think that TV show will air on TV.

Cher: Really? All of a sudden after 3 episodes of watching the 4400- you are an expert on predicting the future?
Sonny: I'm not saying I'm an expert. I am just making an educated guess-.

Cher: I believe it will be in November-2014. Yes. The fall season is when it will air.
Sonny: First of all, you know all television shows air in the fall season, and you also know that it will take a year to get signed and all the material written!

Cher: Okay forget it. If you could be any super hero who would you want to be?
Sonny: I would want to be Superwoman.

Cher: Really?
Sonny: I thought you would've picked Wolverine or Robert Downey Jr as the super conceited man.

Cher: He's super cute for an older dude- but not holdin my super power.
Sonny: Super woman is hot, sexy and she has everything she

could ever want.

Cher: Yeah- yeah. I want to be a person with great memory recall, this way I can be 89 years old and no-one can treat me bad because I would remember and do something about it!

Sonny: That's boring. When you are old you are still old. Why not aim for youth for your super power then?

Cher: That sounds good. I could deal with forever youngness!

Sonny: That's not a word!

Cher: In text language it is. YUNGNES.

Sonny: *Everything* in text language *is* a word.

Cher: Are you ready to go find out how to- get or make our super power emerge tonight?

Sonny: I am ready. I can't wait to check out that place. We are going to have fun. I'll bet you that I will be the most powerful one there once we get going.

Cher: Powerful – you mean talented or gifted? Because I do believe there is a difference between powerful and gifted. It's really a huge difference between the two words.

Sonny: Blah balah balah. That's all I hear from you.

Cher: I'm getting sleepy.

Sonny: You just said you were going to be the most powerful "one" there tonight.

Cher: I will after we get me a Chai latte. All the carbs in that pasta make me *sleepy*.

Sonny: Okay you will get your precious Chai latte and I will join you- it's truly the after dinner drink of champions.

After Dinner

That night after Sonny and Cher's 2nd dinner, they drove to that

32

local mindful center. They joined the workshop on *how to read auras and energy*. They got their just in the nick of time. The class started promptly at 8pm. The teacher introduced herself as a spiritual teacher and psychic. She explained to the 11 person class that they would learn how to sense and feel energy vibrations. They would also learn how to decipher positive energy from negative energy in a person's electromagnetic field.

Cher loved that the spiritual teacher went into detail about Chakras. The teacher said they were in every human and everything that exists contains energy. She gave all the students facts and then gave her opinion without forcing any belief system on them.

Sonny continued to be a smart ass and ask a million questions. The spiritual teacher happily obliged by giving details such as:

Chakras are energy centers that are located down the center of a person's body along the meridian or spinal column. These wheel or discs like centers are also associated with colors for each chakra point. There are 7 main chakras but there are over 144,000 chakras in the human body. These are energy centers that constantly open and close on a day to day basis. She said they are spiral-like and flow in and out of the body form.

Each chakra represents a center point in the human body which can energize, release, hold or vibrate. Of which, these energy centers constantly open and close during the day. This is normal, but keeping them balanced is the key to being a balanced human. When I say balanced, I mean psychically, mentally emotionally and spiritually balanced.

When humans are unbalanced in any one of these areas they can be over compensating in another area of the body. If a chakra is out of place- for a long period of time, sickness can manifest. This could be as physical, mental, emotional or spiritual. So keeping *yourself* and your energy centers /chakras aligned and

33

balanced is a must. The class really liked when the teacher stood up and showed them with a huge drawing of where the Chakras were located on the human body. It was a color coded diagram; it was easy to understand the concept.

She pointed at the drawing and showed them the chakra at the base of the spine is called the root or 1st chakra. This chakra represents 'grounding". The 2nd chakra is named the sacral - representing "survival, instinct", the 3rd chakra is solar plexus representing "personal power or EGO.

The 4th chakra -the heart, representing love and compassion. The 5th chakra is the throat chakra representing communication, expression, and creativeness and also listening.

The 6th chakra representing the "third eye" or mind's eye. This represents intuitiveness and trusting in yourself.

Lastly is the 7th chakra- which represents connection to your higher self and other beings of light. This higher –self is the all knowing you-you can connect with the celestial plane of Angels, Spirit guides, and humans that have passed over or on other dimensions.

She explained knowing more about your physical, emotional and mental body is an excellent way of certain balance or energy exchange with yourself on level that is physical and mental along with spiritually. Taking good care of your physical body is part of the exchange as well. You most likely feel healthier or "better" when you eat foods that are known as natural or organic, basically unprocessed. That is a positive energy exchange with your insides and outside on the physical level. Your chakras are the example of the perfect energy exchange on an energetic level.
 The teacher then went on to say that the human aura works in synchronicity with our energy centers. Chakras and auras work together for balancing our human bodies.

She told the class that energy sessions are a healthy alternative method for cleansing the energy in one's body. She said to think of it as a monthly maintenance.

One method she spoke of is a modality of *energy healing* called Reiki to keep our bodies' aura clean and clear. She said the clarity keeps people aligned and balanced feeling great.

Sonny sure shut her trap after that long winded explanation from the psychic teacher. Sonny usually would interrupt, but was really listening and taking notes.

Later the psychic teacher took the whole class into a big open room in the Mindful center. Sonny and Cher said it was very interesting. They described the details that there were lots of paintings on the walls that she claimed carry energy from Angels. The paintings were colorful and each one had very different styles to them.
When Sonny asked the teacher about them, she explained that she channeled each painting. That spirits came through her body as if she was in a trance state of mind. Each painting was energy art and gave a message. They were for humans to use as tools to self-heal their physical, mental or emotional bodies. The teacher claimed: These *mandalas are sacred geometry*. Cher was impressed. The psychic teacher said each painting could be used for advancing humans in their current life.

Of course Cher wanted *in* -on this. She thought this could be the start of *her* super powers. She pictured her body becoming a weapon or something incredible that no other human could possess! This of course, is what she thought in her mind.

Cher picked out a painting that was for advancing her with direction in her life-. Sonny laughed while Cher decided to purchase a print to meditate with after the workshop was over that night. Sonny on the other hand, also decided to purchase a mandala painting to bring more love into her life.

Everyone at the workshop that night - according to Cher felt the energy from these paintings. She described it as feeling tingles from the art. Hot and tingly-that's what she said. She felt it from her hands and finger tips and a bit in her arms. The Mindful Center sold several reprints of the energy paintings to each student that night. The teacher did a mini presentation of how to place crystals and gemstones on the mandala paintings to increase the energy that each would emit. This amplified energy of the crystals placed on top and would move the energy flow into our human aura.

Both girls loved this place. They said they had so much to learn. It was different and new and they thought it would be great to know this kind of lifestyle for their creative writing.

They hung for an hour after the workshop was over and talked to a few older women they met during class. They sat at the tea bar inside the Mindful Center had some Chai tea and joked around. They all planned on coming back the following Thursday for the manifesting workshop.

Both Sonny and Cher went home and watched season two of 4400 till they fell asleep.

A few days went by until they met again for dinner.

Dinner Number Three Tres

Once again Sonny met Cher at the restaurant around 6pm. It was dinner number 3. Sonny wanted to share more of her short stories to Cher and Cher wanted to talk about dating.

Sonny: What do you think?
Cher: About what?

Sonny: About *me* -becoming a psychic interviewer.

Cher: What are you talking about?
Sonny: Tonight after class I'm going to ask our psychic teacher if I can interview her. Do you think she's say yeahas?

Cher: I would say yes. Yes, because I looked on her website and she has been on radio show and many interviews- I'm sure it's nothing new to her and why not- you are the famous Blahhhhhhhhhhhhhhhh writer Haahahah!
Sonny: Oh well *thank you* -my kind friend- now *bow to me* as I get up to go pee.

Cher: Want me to order for us?
Sonny: Please do. My servant.

Dev: Hi. How are you? Ready for drinks?
Cher: Yes, we just want water with lemon and both will have our same order again. Do you remember the ingredients?
Dev: Of course- it's the weird, I mean interesting combo with a fried egg- no prob. And you both like hot water with lemon. I'll be back.

Sonny: I'm baaaack!
Cher: All orders in. And yes, he looks deliscioso tonight.
Sonny: Oh Dev- yeah, well that goes without saying.

Cher: Have you written any new stuff?

Sonny: Yep. I keep working with that energy art I bought and I have been feeling a lot of emotions.

Cher: Oh yes. The mandala you bought from the psychic lady.
Sonny: You got one too!

Cher: Emotions? Is that good or bad? Hey switching subjects- If psychic teach lets me interview her, do you think she'd be pissed if I ask her about some crazy chit? Ya know like I usually ask my South Beach and TV crowd?

 Sonny: Please don't be that person. Why don't you wait till we are done learning what we want first? And what about me. MY Emotions!

 Dev: Hi. So do you both plan on coming every Thursday now? I mean I just noticed that you have been coming a few weeks in a row. I don't mean to pry- but do you work around here?

Cher: OH, well we do some work here and there. We go to some workshops close to here and we figure why not eat at this restaurant because *it's got food.*
Dev: Oh Okay. Yeah I understand. Cool. Okay I'll be back when the dinners are ready.

Sonny: You dork! You made us sound like idiots! He was trying to small talk and be nice to us!
Cher: I didn't want him to know why we *really* here.
 I do like that he remembers we like hot waters and lemon. It's sweet.

Sonny: Uggghh . You are so- NOT smooth.
Cher: No wonder we are both single.

 Sonny: I won't be for long- after tonight, I'm manifesting a man.
Cher: Are you going to read me any of your short stories tonight at dinner?

Sonny: Well Okay. If- you insist. I have a pretty good one. I wrote this a few nights ago. Here ya go:

 I call it: Atlantis 2051

The frequency of what you know of this planet has changed throughout history.

This particular planet was one that held liquid. It was pure and of the highest vibrational frequency.

As our history states this planet had an extreme occurrence that changed the atmosphere- Splitting and brought a divination of its existence. When this happened two dimensions were created. This means there became 2 separate places of this "planet".

The cause of the splitting of the frequencies- the planet became two separate places- two separate dimensions that were at that moment became a parallel of each other.

One parallel dimension was of liquidity. This water-named place is *Atlantis*.

The inhabitants were named *light beings* due to their abilities to emit the high frequencies.

The other- became a place they called *Earth*- it was the other parallel dimension. It became a consistency of liquid and land. It contained *people*.

The split was not intentional- the atmosphere divided .

Then, again over history-another change occurred.

One of the parallels changed in a great decline in their frequency It began to emit low vibrations- due to conditional occurrences- such as pollution, toxins and low vibrancies of the existence that resided on that parallel. They colonized "people." These were creatures that inhabited that parallel. These people also created vibrations. Sadly, overall, they created low vibrancy.

This derived from the people's inner working parts of which they called *thoughts and verbalization*. Best described as "sadness and greed"- this brought a quick decline of the parallel. There- on Earth parallel-these *people* filled the space with negative energy exchanges and their lower vibrancy emissions overtook the positive people's vibrancies.

At that point earth the land and liquid place transformed into only liquid. This caused less and less people that inhabited the earth parallel. As the changes occurred it became an amphibious place. Many of the people adapted to this liquid positive frequency-they called this new "air".

Once again, the Earth parallel and the Atlantis parallel went back to natural order- whereas in dot point.2051 there became an interchange of frequencies a combination of both places to become one.

Now -we only know that this place called earth is a myth yet to be proven, but Atlantis is still out in our cosmos. As you can view my child- you can look down and see it approximately every 28 turns.

Sonny: What do ya think?

Cher: I like it –very interesting the whole theory stuff. But what the heck is the dot. Point thing? What is that?

Sonny: I thought that made it sound like star treck-y.

Cher: No. Not at all. I'd skip that. Dot. Dot. Dot. Point- dumb!

Sonny : Once again I appreciate your loving input. Can you see my middle finger?
Cher: You need to take it seriously- 'I'm just trying to help. I am not trying to make you feel bad.

Sonny: I know. Okay I have one more. This one was really weird for me because it was a vivid dream. I felt like I was our psychic teacher. I mean like I *was her* in this dream *and I felt* all these things. Okay, I am just going to read what I wrote as I woke up:

I was finishing up a psychic reading for a woman asking about her son and her relationship with him. I started to feel jumpy as I watched her lips open and clamp down while she was talking to me. We were in a private session. My heart began to beat really fast- I figured since I can sense and feel things from other people- I assumed I was feeling the woman that was in front of me in the reading session.

I felt her nervousness as she kept talking. I felt the boom, boom of her heart beat. It actually hurt the inside of my chest. When I was channeling messages the client usually listens to me- but this lady wanted to talk. It was like a release for her. She was putting energy out with her voice- the vibrations were strong. She just needed to let it out and say it verbally to someone.

As the session wrapped up- I continued to feel jumpy- my heart was still fast beating and I begun to have a cold sweat. I imagined in my mind to let go of all this woman's uncertainties and energy that was shaken. I tried to imagine all of that different energy going out of my body – out of my energy field into the earth to be recycled by mother earth. At that time, I realized I had 17 people in the next room waiting for me to perform guided meditation.

I said my goodbyes to that lady client and prepared for the group meditation. Everyone all 17 were sitting down and ready to start. I spoke slowly and calmly as I asked them to close their eyes. I guided them all to imagine and visualize happiness. I started by mentioning colors of gold and blue and took them to a relaxing place. I described a mountain top that was peaceful and safe.

I then led them to breathe in love and exhale any toxins or negative thoughts out of their bodies. This was to clean and clear their body and mind. I spoke softly as I advised them to follow - then suddenly I wanted to barf! I grabbed my stomach- sat on the floor and prayed to the Angels to help me! Everyone's eyes

41

were closed and I felt as if each person appeared to be in a serene place in their minds while meditating.

I didn't want to alarm anyone- as my heart beat went from zero to a zillion per minute. It was so fast I felt like a 2 ton elephant stomped on my back *and* front of my chest at the same time.

I gasped for air on the floor in a kneeling position. I kept praying that everyone in the room would only feel love from Angels and not my pain.

As I prayed to make it through this session without anyone feeling my pain- about 6 minutes later- I stood and was able to finish the meditation smoothly without anyone knowing my episode. I completed the mediation by saying "focus on your third eye, now your throat, the center of your heart and moving down to the stomach area feel the love and energy in your bodies- as you bring your attention to your solar plexus feel your strength, and the sacral chakra imagine an orange ball of light- now focus on the base of your feet- connect into the ground with mother earth and be balanced."

I completed the meditation. The session was over everyone then opened their eyes at a slow pace. Some people grounded into their bodies quicker than others. I knew as always the group and I would share what we felt or saw in our minds eyes during the meditation- many shared that they saw colors or released a negative thought. Overall, everyone said they all felt wonderful.

I was so glad no-one had picked up what I felt. After the group left the center- I was still feeling super cold chills and my hands freezing. It felt like iceberg cold. Although I was super sweaty my backside felt frozen. I turned all the utilities off and I locked the store for the night. I quickly drove home to lie down.

I knew it was heart attack. Just days before I wrote a monologue of a woman same age as me having a heart attack – I guess I was warning myself...a message.

That night I took some aspirin. I never take any pharmas- but tonight I felt I had no choice. I lay down and prayed for life- as the strong migraine pain came over my face, neck and shoulders. My chest felt heavy and had a stabbing pain- again I felt nauseous and sick-but after 6 aspirins I finally slept.

The next morning I went to a medical walk- in clinic to get an EKG test.

Later that same day –a brown box was delivered to my door. It was a box with sneakers I ordered from zappos. I was so dead tired I could barely move. I saw the mail carrier dropped it by the front door. I saw the package from my window. I forced my legs to move to walk to my door and get the package and bring it inside my house. I wanted to open it but my hands couldn't open the packing tape. I was freaking weak as a willow.

After a few hours of lying around on the couch- I got a knife and cut the box open. No surprise it was my new black sneaks I ordered online. I placed them on the floor and walked to go to the bathroom.

When I returned to the couch- in the middle of my floor was a grey feather- I saw a feather. No idea how it got there but it was in plain sight to find.

I picked the feather from the floor and grabbed my cell to google-"Is a feather an omen?"
I read a few websites that a psychic shared that a feather means *"a message is coming – or death."* As an intuitive, I was open to other people's opinions.

I had found feathers before- each time it was around a death of someone -or a client that had come to me to communicate to a deceased loved one in a session.

This had me upset. I started to think maybe it was for my own death?

43

Shit. Now I was really going to have a hard time sleeping. I really had no doubt that *I did* have a heart attack- it runs in my family both sides.

I felt like I was age 42 and I predicted my own death of a heart attack. Oddly enough when I teach I explain there is no – time – since people/humans created the clock. I tell them I believe in parallel dimensions as many scientists agree- but calculations could be wrong since time is just the moment or an occurrence that one experiences.

Tired of thinking scenarios- I finally went into a deep sleep- it may have been the 5 or 6 aspirins I swallowed out of fear.

I woke up at 3:33am. I felt a presence – I remembered my dream. The place I was wonderful. My old/ex- boyfriend from when I was 17 appeared. He took me to an outside eatery- we laughed and joked-It was normal and nice. I saw that he was the same age as me in this vision. He was 42 too.

He told me that the feather I saw earlier that day on my floor in my home was from him! I felt relived. We continued to talk to other people in my dream. We met two young girls selling grilled veggies from a food cart. We sat and chatted with them and ate. Then my ex excused himself to go to the men's room. As he turned to go into the men's room I had a feeling it was time for him to go- and the dream was ending. I opened my mouth and the words I said to him were "I'm choosing to stay." Then I immediately woke up.
Short story over!

Cher: Wow! You really were the psychic teacher in that dream. Do you think that was something that really happened to her? Or do you think it was your crazy imagination?
Sonny: I don't know but it was so real- I felt like her. Should I ask her or tell her what I dreamed?

Cher: Well, you might freak her out with the heart attack thing. But you have had a few of your short stories with heart issues in your character. That's fawked up. Maybe it's a message you are going to die from a heart attack in the future.

Sonny: I know. What? Do you think it's about me? No. It can't be. *I'm Superwoman.*
 I don't want her to think I'm a psycho path or trying to take over her soul or something like that.
Cher: Well, I would keep it to yourself for now. No sense in being a Freak!

Both Sonny and Cher ate their dinner as usual and left a big tip for their hottie Dev.
 They drove over to the Mindful Center for the manifesting class starting at 8pm. This night there was 22 people in the class. Cher was really surprised since the location of where the classes were held was really small and hard to find.

When the spiritual teacher talked about how to manifest- the whole group was writing everything down. She had the total class's undivided attention. She taught everyone in the class to manifest money, jobs, health, *and* the one that most interested Sonny and Cher was manifesting a "good match."

Cher thought it was funny when the teacher told them a soul mate could be anyone- that she could be Cher's soul mate. She used it as an example to make her point. She said *we are all souls that live together*- so all of us are soul mates- since we all live on earth.
Good matches are those people in our lives that are usually long term and bring marriage or true connections with respecting each other in many ways. They accept each other's normal and are truly happy.

45

They said this night just got better and better. They learned how to manifest pretty much anything they wanted. They got all the details on how to manifest a good match described as a male counterpart that is best suited for them in this lifetime. They did learn that a person can have more than one good match in a lifetime which Cher found very interesting to say the least. Sonny wrote down exactly how to manifest this significant other. Her notes were:

Manifesting a "Good Match"

Take 3 long breaths in and 3 exhales out. At my own pace. Sit in a place I feel comfortable and peaceful, indoors or outdoors. Try to feel my heart. Focus by holding my hands lightly over my chest area. I can do this with both my hands. Now understand that my body and mind are now connected.

Continue with my focus on "Asking equally" to manifest my man my good match.

I can state this aloud or within. If I need to stop and get a paper and pen to write or add more details-please do this. Make sure I'm manifesting accordingly.
I am and I allow myself to meet a man -I don't need a name) that has healthy habits, that is respectful to me and I to him. He is attracted to me sexually, intellectually, physically and emotionally and I to him. We love each other 100%; we are monogamous to each other .We communicate properly and nicely to each other, we understand each other's feelings and way of thinking. We accept each other's "normal", we are happy together and trust each other. We are each other's good match and we deserve each other. We meet November 2014-Now, now now! (I can insert a month and year then say earth dimension.

Other options I can use
my man would have a good paying job or owner

He is humorous and courteous to me
He has values similar mine or values I admire.

He is available (not married!) to meet me
We both have compatible "normals and accept each other's "normal"
He is specifically good looking example: tall, physically fit, green eyes and Hot.
He is abundant in money
He is psychically healthy, emotionally sound.

A Note- Remember!!! The Angels said, "I can't be someone's "good match, if I'm not his. This is equal energy exchange."

Both young ladies agreed that they would meet their *good match* by the end of November. It was currently October 28. They sure dedicated themselves to meeting their dream man sooner than later.

After the manifesting class was over- Cher asked the psychic teacher if she would like to do an interview for *Blah* magazine. The teacher was excited and agreed. They were to meet the following morning for the formal interrogation- I mean interview.

That same night, at 10pm they were in the Mindful Center parking lot. Sonny and Cher stood outside under the stars and made a bet. Cher bet Sonny she would meet her good *match* earlier than Cher. Yep, the bet was for 60 bucks.

They also said something that was incredibly ridiculous. They said they would meet men at a tea or coffee houses. A total of 6 dates with men- each. They would meet the men from dating sites and a new APP where you can look at the men's faces and pick him solely from his looks. They went on to further explain the rules of their bet.

While one was on a date, the other lady would sit in the same coffee place at another table. They then would spy on each other's coffee dates.

Both would try to read the aura and energy of the man on the date. Then afterwards Sonny and Cher would meet at their favorite restaurant. This was to be done every Thursday night. They would coordinate the men to meet them at 6pm at the coffee location, stay 30 minutes and then both would meet at the order by number restaurant by 6:45pm.

I know this is kinda entertaining- but at the same time it is really sick. The poor guys- it is like someone is invading their privacy in just a weird way!
The creepiness of this is unsettling.

Both ladies were taught that same week at the Mindful center from their psychic teacher that respecting others space and privacy was a rule of proper energy exchanges.

These bets they placed about people's energy is just not kosher. Their teacher said it was invading privacy and it would be like someone walking in on them in the bathroom without knocking on the door- super *uncool*. It was definitely a bad energy exchange from both ladies.

That was their newest bet and event.

These ladies wanted to do more research on medium ship and channeling. As it be- there was a workshop during the week at the Mindful center- and they signed up for the workshop before they left that night.

After their game plans were discussed in the parking lot, both ladies went home for the night. Of course, after performing their fake Vulcan-like hand sign to each other as they drove away.

The Interview

That next morning, Cher met her psychic teacher at 11 am at the Mindful Center. They sat and had tea served to them from a volunteer working the tea bar. Cher set up her tape recorder and her notes she spilled her tea on her shirt and just pretended it didn't happen since it was a minuet amount of liquid.

Cher had a way about her that was nice, but she could also ask some questions that are totally off the wall and nothing relating to the interview. That was her quirky style. Cher's opening question to her teacher was …if her family thought she was crazy and how did she know she has psychic abilities.

The answers she received were well versed by the psychic teacher and she could tell she had been asked this same question many times. The psychic teacher would smirk and have a slight laugh after every stupid question Cher asked her.

Cher asked about other abilities namely telepathic communication. The psychic teacher taught online classes and had a theory on telepathy. "The theory of the Tele- box." The psychic teacher actually gave her written sheet of paper of an outline of what she teaches about it- in hopes Cher would get the concept without any mistakes.
These were the exact notes:

The Theory of the Tele- box
The purpose of this box is to be a location point is to communicate telepathically with messages that are eventually

utilized by the masses.

This "tele-box" is open to receive and transmit the vibrations that are input or received from the box.

This tele-box theory is that vibration of thoughts; visions and "words with meaning" are sent and placed in these boxes which hold these vibrations using strong thought patterns which are vibrations.

Anyone with telepathic abilities can vibrationally sync up with the vibrations in the box to receive the message or messages that were placed there.

In years to come humans will use this tele-box to leave and pick up messages to and from another- similar to text messages and or voice mail.

Mind to mind communications have been practiced for many years, but tuning in constantly can become energetically annoying.

If many *calls* were *incoming* at once into the human mind these messages can be mixed or bring confused outcomes of the messages or visions sent.

That is why the tele -box works without human error. One must trust the frequency of the message from the sender to decipher it correctly and receive and interpret the message accurately.

Theories

The first theory is to place one message, a simple one word message in this location called the tele-box- which holds the vibrations.

My study: Inviting 20 people to "tune 'in to the vibrations of this tele- box and hear or sense the message via visions, thought or feeling this message.

The second study is to use this box as a drop of vibrations, meaning the 20 people would sync vibrations to connect and receive the message that was placed in that location, and then leave another message in its place of vibrancy.

As this is occurring each of the 20 waits their turn to sync up to the message, receive it, and then place a new vibrancy message for the next person, until all 20 have done this procedure. This test will allow us to work toward using a Place or location- a vortex of messages, using a location point similar to mail boxes for paper mail.

We can also compare this to the Morse code that transmitted code with sound of clicking beeps. This mechanism proved to send and transmit identified messages.

Now advanced humans can identify vibrations that match this energy center- the tele-box. When syncing one would make connections to a specific place/tele box to receive vibrational messages that can be in forms of vibrations such as: thought vibrancies, sensing or feeling from emotional vibrancies, visual vibrancies, and /or verbal words.

This tele-box can be:
1) a location point on earth, for example: an address such as longitude and latitude,
2)a person- since humans are perfect conduits and are made of energy- humans are made up of vibrations containing vortexes
3)or a mandala- a physical or mental picture a visualization-a vortex that was specifically identified with intent as the "box location".

The reasoning behind the mandala box was inspired from energies other than earth bound- I clairaudiently heard messages that were channeled through me- to create this mandala painting for the sole purpose that it would be used by humans to communicate telepathically from one human mind to another. As the earth changes due to cosmic events, humans are affected

51

by vibrational morphing. In the future this will peak approximately the years 2021-2025 will be the peak of adhering to this new way of communication mind to mind.

This is not to say humans will not be able to speak- human's will- but as we evolve into a higher frequency vibrations from the changes in the atmosphere people will be able to "connect" without devices that are cumbersome such as cellular phones during those years on earth.

This is an amazing cultivation of human life- I am currently practicing and teaching mind skills to tele-communicate with other people worldwide and I look forward to the years to come of advancement of humankind.

To learn and practice tele-communication you can join the worldwide telepathic team.
http://www.The AcademyofTelepathy.com

*Strengthen your communication skills
*increase your brain functionality
* preparation for the future

Cher quickly looked over the papers on the tele- theory the blonde psychic teacher gave her and placed them in her blue folder and continued the interview. Cher asked these questions below and got these answers from the psychic teacher:

Cher: Can I call you a psychic teacher?

Psychic teacher: Sure-or *intuitive* is also good.
Cher: I'm recording this. Is that okay with you?

Psychic teacher: Yes, that is fine.
 Cher: Thank you for meeting me. The magazine I work for is kind of crazy- but I feel this interview would be really cool for people to read and know more about you.

Psychic teacher: I am happy you asked me- I like to reach as many people as I can by sharing information that I receive from the light. The information is to help people move forward and give them guidance for choosing the right path- the right path for them at that particular moment in their life. Ultimately advancing them and bringing them more happiness and fulfillment in their life.

Cher: I first would like to know, how did you get started in all this psychic stuff? Were your born with it? Did you learn it from someone?

Psychic teacher: Well- I have always had some feelings when I was a young child. I knew spirits existed. I had some friends pass away in my teenage years and I wanted to contact them.
I strongly believe we are all born with intuitiveness.

Cher: How did you do that?

Psychic teacher: I decided to look at a candle flame and ask my deceased friend to make it jump up and down and stop still. Then I would ask him a question -The stop still flame was yes and the jumping flame from the candle was the answer no. That's how I started communicating with the deceased.
Then later I started to auto write messages. That is when it feels like someone you cannot see takes your hand and writes or draws information on paper- my hand would just follow. It's really amazing.

Cher: Wow, that's interesting. Can I- do that?

Psychic teacher: I believe everyone can do that. It just takes an open mind and practice.

Cher: If I wanted you to contact Elvis? Could you do that?

Psychic teacher: Well, I would ask him first. If he wants to talk to you- then go from there. Remember I told you about asking for permission out of respect. Remember- everything is energy.

Cher: How do you feel about the bible? Some people feel psychics are evil and are not good practice for religious reasons.
Psychic teacher: This is an interesting question. First of all, I feel all religions are good. They bring people together and conformity. I feel that all religions have one basic principle in common. It is - that there is a *source* that exists. It could be God, Buddha, Jah, Goddess- any source you call it- him or her- it's just pure positive energy-and *source* is infinite, divine and beautiful. As I believe we are infinite. *Source* is also a label- but I am hoping people see it as politically correct. It's just a label for us as humans to identify something.

In many debates- I have brought up that the bibles of any religion were written documents to keep *order* in the world- along with explaining a story of people or energies of the unknown and unexplainable. Some of what happens in everyday life, but is not always noticed. Some people would call theses occurrences *coincidences.*

Back to the bibles and religion… during certain eras or times, there were moments which people as communities, needed to have order. They may have needed strict rules or apply laws- these beliefs were written to keep people in a good state of thoughts giving them real structure. Structure is good.

As I was saying previously, the bibles could have been written and rewritten – as many stories and rumors change throughout the times from one person to another over time. As the needs of conformity changed throughout time. This could've been due to the way people perceive information or facts. To me this change throughout years and years of the written documents- means it may not be totally accurate.

As I see things- and in my perception in life- there is no wrong- just difference. And differences can be good or not so good depending on who or whom these differences effect.

54

People can argue all day long- but love is love- respect is respect and honor is honor. It is the *definition* and *meaning* of these powerful words that I hope one day are felt, seen, noticed and taught as the *same* for all humans- all life. Just keepin it all positive.

To each his own. That is my favorite quote. I know I went a couple directions in explaining my opinions- I guess it's because I believe everything is good until it harms. ..

Cher: That is a great answer. I get what you are saying... I think it's a cool way of looking at it. And it's very interesting that you feel all religion is good.

Cher: Do you think you are special because you have insight that is beyond other peoples?

Psychic teacher: Absolutely not. We are all equal. Everyone has gifts- everyone is able to utilize psychic abilities as I mentioned before- it's just who allows it and accepts it for the greater good.

Cher: Could you give me one of your best stories of your life?

Psychic teacher: Okay, but its long.

Cher: I am cool with that- fire away.

Psychic teacher: This is a story about me. I cannot share anything I hear or say with my clients- since that is confidential information. I hope one of my personal stories is interesting enough for what you are looking for.

When I was a teenager, I wanted badly to be an actress. When I moved to Florida for college - I was going to castings in Miami. I had local modeling and minor jobs here and there.

For example one time I got called for this infomercial-you know to model a dress that was called the "infinite" dress. You could wear it 8 different ways and it was all one piece of material! That infomercial was hilariously funny. They had a before and after picture on video of me. Before they actually placed dark circles

55

under my eyes with make-up. The after photo I was made-up perfectly. Perfect hair, perfect make-up- perfect dress! When it aired usually late at night my friends up north in Jersey saw me in the commercial – no lie at 3am in the morning!

That year, I was doing some infomercial ads for jewelry, fanny packs, exercise equipment and all sorts of stuff- it was fun. I'd make a few hundred bucks here and there-But my true dream- was to be famous as an actress.

One night when I was out playing pool and drinking with my lifeguard boyfriend at the time- I had something happen to me. I was close to drunk and my boyfriend was trying to mess with my mind. I assume he thought it was funny. He was as drunk as I and wanted to start shit. He told me that this older couple in the bar was staring at me and said they were swingers or something. He told me that I should tell them to stop looking at me. I was quite naive at that time and came from a town that kept me kind of in the dark, especially of matter of this kind.

Basically he sure did a great job on scaring me that night. He had me so upset the moment that couple came over to me to say "hello", I snubbed them and ran across the bar.

All of a sudden, I felt my body, but I also believed I left my body. I know this is hard to explain. I can describe it as an out of body experience. I saw my body as if I was looking at me from a distance. When that occurred, I saw that my personality- my aura and my energy looked ugly that night.

Normally I was a happy, funny person to be with. That night I was ugly and distorted by alcohol. Later that night, about an hour or so, I went home. Of course slept off my buzz and surly had a hangover. My roommate was one that reads the newspaper on Sundays. She opened up the newspaper and I saw the couple that was trying to say "hello" to me kindly that night before. They were scouts for hiring young actors for a TV series. It was a show that ran for many seasons. If I told you the name you'd say... you would not believe me. Never-the-less one of my many lessons was that having distorted energy is disrespecting me and others. I also learned to be more trusting in others until they prove otherwise. If I did- I would have known the true intentions they have with me. Because intentions can differ - and that does not mean I should judge. My energy was distorted because I drank alcohol. This was a lesson for me.

 I lost a grand opportunity – A great chance at my dream - but in the long run I know today that – the lessons I learned were far more valuable than being cast on that TV show. Although it would've been nice! But seriously- looking back I wasn't ready for that- It would've been bad timing for me. I know this now.

 Cher: Wow. I like that story. You sure you won't tell me *what* TV show? Come on you can tell me the name of it...-Just kidding I won't dig.

The psychic teacher laughed at Cher because she knew that Cher really *did* want to dig.
Cher went on and on asking the psychic teacher an array of unrelated questions after that last one. It was a 2 hour interview. In hindsight Cher explained that she probably asked many of the questions for her own curiosity not just for the article she would submit. At least she owned –up on that.

Tuesday Night

The workshop on channeling and mediumship was Tuesday. Sonny and Cher met at the Mindful Center and grabbed some good seats. The place was packed- channeling was a big draw. Everyone was given a handout of the outline of class. The psychic teacher told everyone she copied this information from a website she admired.

The credits to the website were available on the handout- if they wanted to check the site on our own time.

After the workshop the ladies booked a double private session for the following morning with their psychic teacher to learn more about channeling and some other interesting views about other subjects related. They went to the front desk and prepaid.

Wednesday Morning

Sonny and Cher met with the psychic teacher at the mindful center once more. They wanted to get some more extensive knowledge on channeling, mediumship and other stuff like crystal meditations. They felt it would help them with their writing projects. They knew this information would be perfect especially for the television shows or a fiction book. They were both hoping *and* betting each other to win! Especially to win that book writing contest.

They booked 2 hours of time to absorb all they could. The psychic teacher charged them minimally since she believes that mentorship is one of the best ways to bring harmony and spread the words of the light. The ladies simultaneously put their quotation fingers in the air when they told me the teacher said "knowledge is king."

Both ladies took extensive notes, of all the *"knowledge"* their teacher spoke.

They were going to add-on another few hours but the psychic teacher was already booked with another client. They decided that the following morning on Thursday- they would all meet again. Sonny and Cher wanted to know *more* about crystals and their healing energies.

Here are some interesting things... Cher found the website about meduimship and copied this information: Her credits are noted from http://www.fst.org/medium2.htm

Cher said she secretly desired to be a medium, but was "not into meeting any discarnate energies!"

Medium ship
Channeling

Mediumship can be defined as follows: The process whereby a human instrument, known as a MEDIUM or CHANNEL, is used by one or more discarnate, spirit personalities for the purpose of:

- Presenting information, verifiable or otherwise.
- Causing so-called paranormal activities to occur.
- Channeling forth certain types of energies.
- Manifesting themselves for objective examination and/or identification.

- Mediumship involves a cooperating effort between a person on the Earth plane (the medium or channel) and a person in Spirit (the communicator).
- There are several objectives behind the manifestation of mediumship.

In addition to this, we see that mediumship is used by those in Spirit for the following purposes:

- To present information, which may or may not be verifiable.
- To cause certain types of paranormal activities to occur.
- To channel forth certain types of energies.
- To manifest themselves materially.

Therefore, mediumship involves the cooperation between at least two individuals:

- An Earth-plane channel or medium
- A spirit communicator or operator.

You will note that we distinguish between a spirit communicator and a spirit operator.

If you look at what has been said, thus far, concerning mediumship, you will see that two distinct types of phenomena can occur through mediums:

- Communication
- Manipulation of energies and energy systems.

A spirit, who uses a medium for the purpose of communication, either verbally or visually, is known as a spirit communicator. A spirit who uses a medium for the intent of working with and/or manipulating energies or energy systems is called a spirit operator. This distinction is very general, and it should be noted that a spirit operator can, and often does, communicate.

Thus, mediumship can be distinguished as two basic types:

- Mental Mediumship
- Physical Mediumship

Mental mediumship involves the relating of information, through communication, via the varied aspects of thought transference, or mental telepathy. Mental telepathy is the relaying of information via thought, without using any of the five physical senses. Mental mediumship takes place within the consciousness of the medium. The results are expressed verbally and must pass through the medium's mouth. Because of its telepathic nature, mental mediumship is sometimes referred to as telepathic mediumship.

In a demonstration of mental mediumship, it is the medium that hears, sees, and feels what the spirit communicators are relating. Furthermore, it is the medium's function to relate the information, with minimum personal influence and prejudice, to the recipient of the message, also known as the sitter. The medium receives this information under various states of control.

Physical mediumship involves the manipulation and transformation of physical systems and energies. The spirit operators, in this case, are causing something to happen upon the Earth plane. What it is that actually happens varies with the style of mediumship involved, but the results can be seen and heard by others.

Thursday morning –Another double appointment with the psychic teacher

11 am sharp- they all met at the Mindful center. Sonny and Cher had their trusty notebooks and i-pads. They were sipping their lattes from Dunkin D.
They never went anywhere without the note taking devices or their lattes. Their psychic teacher greeted them and brought them inside the Mindful center. They walked into a room that was way in the back. It was past the tea bar area. It was a blue room with the walls covered with paintings she had channeled. The teacher asked them to sit comfortably on the floor.

 She asked them if they wanted to do crystal meditation before they started to get them in a good state of mind to learn. They were up for that and both agreed.

The teacher said this was a meditation for clarity on their soul's purpose. And since people have more than one purpose they would ask only for one purpose at this time in their life- this would give them good direction of what they need to do to focus on the current purpose they each had .

Cher was wondering if their psychic teacher was reading their minds or tuning in telepathically. Since Cher felt that strong connection to her. It was uncanny how their teacher suggested these meditations, when the ladies were previously talking about their many ideas and trying to focus to get them done.

The meditation started as the psychic teacher guided them to close their eyes and breathe deeply in and deeply out 11 times. Cher was lying down on some fluffy cushions made of colorful materials and Sonny sat Indian style with her back against the wall with a single green pillow.

Between them the teacher placed a large round cushion. It looked like a foot rest only comfy-like. She then placed a golden colored mandala painting on top of the large cushion. The painting was a square shape and looked like it was approximately 16x16 in size. The teacher placed it with care as if she was honoring it or it was a prize procession.

They were told this painting was channeled for humans to find clarity on their soul's purpose. They both breathed in and deeply out 11 times- at a very slow relaxed pace. They both felt calm. They started to feel light in their physical bodies and in their minds went somewhere visually different than in that small back room where they were actually sitting. It was similar to what Sonny experienced in her dream- when she thought she was in the psychic teacher's body.

Cher and Sonny let go of their thoughts and began to focus solely on the painting that was placed between them on the large cushion, as directed by the teacher. Sonny and Cher were instructed to place their hands over this gold painted mandala. This was part of the process in the meditation.
They claimed it had a strong vibration both ladies said they felt some kind of tingly sensations in their entire bodies. Sonny described it as "movement "in and around her body. At this point both Sonny and Cher had their eyes shut. The teacher expressed she was placing crystals on top of the golden mandala painting. She instructed them to open their eyes for a few moments and gaze with their hands over the painting with the crystal that was placed on top of it. When they slowly opened

their eyes they saw a combination of green tourmaline and clear quartz crystal strategically placed on the golden mandala. At that point, the teacher turned on a small air diffuser to spread the aroma of fresh rosemary in the room. She said it helps connect to the *"all knowing you- the soul- or higher-self of a human."* The psychic teacher took a huge breath in and they followed her lead, the teacher strongly let her breath out and made sure the ladies knew it was to be done that same way.

Cher's mind went to a *pizzeria-* since rosemary brought her to a thought of food. She then focused to connecting with the gold colored painting with crystals on it. The teacher called it a crystal grid. The psychic teacher spoke softly and asked both Sonny and cher to connect to the light and imagine a string of white light above their heads- she said that was an energetic string that would connect them to their true soul. This would then allow then to hear, feel or sense higher knowledge- information that was from the all-knowing she called "source."

She told them to allow themselves to let go into a connection, not to fight it but to only accept without thoughts and divinely notice the messages they may feel or hear.
The room was noiseless. Sonny and Cher described it to be peaceful and then they had very different experiences from the 30 minutes they "let go."

Cher was deep in her meditation – she was completely relaxed and started feeling as if she was somewhere else- other than this backroom in the Mindful center. She explained it as floating upward- then being placed in another time period. She felt it was in the 1800's. She saw all the people around her suffering from malnutrition.

She thought it may have been England or Ireland. She wasn't sure since she's never been to either location in her real life. That

63

life or place she saw in her mind, she had very little food to survive. Almost as if she wanted to surround herself with food- in her real life -something she lacked in that mind meditation situation.

The information Cher shared after the meditation was like a confirmation that she was in the right field of work, since she loved food and was working for Frommerz - eating and writing about it all the time!

Sonny was totally in a different space in her mind. She said her sensations seemed more tingles that sometimes would surge through her body. She felt light and as if there was a bright light wherever she was… She was in the stars- she said she met Galileo. He told her that she needs to aim for the stars. She felt he meant for her to become a star with her writing. She felt it was a message particularly for television since that is where stars are born.

When the psychic teacher started this *souls purpose meditation* she spoke to each Sonny and Cher and asked them to verbally state these words: *"I allow myself to get a clear vision to my soul's purpose at this time in my life…"* The teacher said for them to ask for a clear focus of what guidance or message they needed at this present lifetime.

She then stated the name of the current month and the year for both Sonny and Cher to repeat along with the versed statement.

All and all- Sonny and Cher loved the pre mediation session with their teacher. After that, they were feeling so floaty they just sat and talked about what they felt and envisioned. The rest of the session turned into talking about many of the psychic teacher's experiences of her past meditations. Sonny and Cher loved it.

The psychic teacher explained previously in a workshop – that she believes there are many places humans can be. This meaning that a person's soul energy can be in more than one place at once and humans are multi-dimensional beings. As we as people have souls- and can be more conscious in one life or moment. Basically, we can be in *another place*–at the same moment. These are simultaneous experiences. This she named or calls it *parallel lives*. She said we can perceive them as past lives because we as people put the word "time" on moments or experiences and occurrences.

She said people place labels such as dates, years, minutes, and second or eras- basically segment of life we perceive. Life to her is seen as energy- she says it is endless- it is infinite.
She told the ladies and everyone at that workshop last week. She explained that the energy of people- and all energy that carries a soul are infinite. She believes life is infinite!

She gave a great example so everyone could understand it. She told them in her many mediumship readings- it is evident that she contacted a person, a loved one. A person that was on earth and had died- she likes to use the word "passed" because she says humans never die- just the skin and bones die- the energy the soul lives. She went on as saying "how could I receive information from a deceased loved one that I never met and get detailed information such as a name, favorite location and describe their personality exactly?

This she said through her experience was proof to her that people that "pass" move out of the body but keep the soul spirit and always keeps it infinitely. Mind to mind we can sense hear and connect with frequencies basically vibrations that are heard by those that practice or naturally have abilities to connect on those frequencies- which become contact. Contact brings the information to those that listen; those who choose to hear sense or feel the information.

I love that concept. It really hit home when the girls passed on this to me. It seems their psychic teacher takes the time to let

65

other people pick their view on an opinion- but still get her point out there.

That other night when the teacher was explaining this information to the whole packed class- one lady wanted to speak of her session she had had with a respectable medium to contact a loved one .She said she received information that only her deceased husband and she would know– the woman said the information was detailed.

She claimed it was a confirmation of life beyond Earth- or Earth dimension- whatever you want to name it. Sonny and Cher wanted to talk to that lady but she had to go quickly after that class. Sonny wanted to interview her, but Cher thought that was not very cool since she would be asking her personal information that she may not want to share.

Dinner Number four Quattro

Sonny and Cher went on to talk about their dates at the restaurant. The ladies changed the rules to go on dates all week.

This was their fourth Thursday night dinner. It was really pathetic. They went on dates all week- Starting from last Saturday until Wednesday. They rattle on their experiences:

Sonny: That was awesome! The guy you met was really hot. You know - the one from Monday night. He was a keeper except he had skinny legs. I don't know why he wore shorts.
Cher: I liked him he was really cute. That was Ted. But I read his aura and it was all funky at the top and I felt grey energy around him. So I'm going to pass on him.

Sonny: Maybe he was stoned or something. Our teacher said that grey can mean drugs when seen in the aura.
Cher: I dunno- maybe. Or maybe Ted just had something bad

happen before he came to meet me. Ya know - like a vampire stopped him and sucked the life out of him before he came to the coffee house.

Sonny: You are such an ass-again! So what is your prediction? Will he call for another date?

Cher: If he does I owe you sixty!

Sonny: I believe those sixty smackers- sure gonna be mine! Be---cause---- he called me back already. So you have to cough up some dough.

Cher: Okay. Here's your sixty bucks bitch. What about my guy? I felt he had orange energy- that means he was hot for me, and wanted some lovin-

Sonny- That's what I got too! Yes. For sure. He wanted some action from you.

Cher: Yeah but that ain't happenin.. He was like a Nick Lachet wanna be

Sonny: who's Nick Lachet?

Cher: You know the guy that Jessica Simpson was married to first. He's cute but kinda average at the same time. He is a host on some show now- like E or something like that.

Sonny: Oh. Okay. I bet he *would* call so- you bet against me originally – we will know in the next few days.

I feel I'm looking at a buck twenty my way! Send over the C-note sista!

Cher: This is fun! But I hate losing! On another track- I started my manifesting today. I woke up this morning before work and sat in front of a tree in my backyard and asked the universe to bring me my good match. I used my list I made with my specifics and asked that I would be equal to him as well.

Sonny: Wow, you actually read directions of something- you must be seriously tired of being alone!

Cher: Yeah, I am.

Sonny: Sometimes you remind me of a Pikachu that little cute thing on the video- the one that's getting what she wants!
Cher: You aren't making sense again- time for you to eat your food and shut the hell up.

Sonny: Speaking of bets.... We made a hundred dollar bet on who would win the create space book contest.
 Cher: Well dumb-ass, you know there are also 10,000 other contestants right?

Sonny: You mean 98,000 others- to be exact.
Cher: Oh you! Sometimes I want to jump across and put that fusilli in your lap!

Sonny: Hahahha.. Yeah I know I'm a smart ass.
Cher: Well I hope one of us win. Did you finish your submission yet?

 Sonny: I did mine yesterday.
Cher: I have to finish mine. It has to be 50, 000 words for the manuscript- that's a lot of words!

Sonny: I know. I had a book started but needed to finish it up. But if I had to start from scratch I would have never had enough time before the deadline.

Cher: Let's make a toast – to winning!
 Sonny: To winning $50,200.00!

Cher: Speaking of books, did you read the book I made of "sayings for T-shirts?"
Sonny: Ahhh, hell no. Are you kidding? Can you make a book JUST for T-shirt sayings?

Cher: Yes. You've seen those books 100 ways to do this or that.

What about 20 ways to examine your poo? That's real. I read it.
Sonny: Do you *really want to own that*? Please tell me you are
lying! Ewe.

Cher: Here, see-I made a mini book- I printed it for you to take
home and read. Please- check it –you'll see it will make you
laugh.
Sonny: I guess you are right. *Crap*- literally sells. I did see this
doo doo bird- it was bird crap or cow crap made into shape of a
bird and it had a feathers stuck in to it to look like – who knows
what- and two wiggly fake eyes to make a poop face! Freaking
amazing what people will buy.

55 T-shirt sayings

The T-shirt book of 55 sayings Cher made for Sonny *was r*eal.
She printed out 55 sayings for T-shirts. In the back of the book
was a mini doll size t-shirt that said "I won." In Cher's weird
way she was trying to make a point that she would win the book
contest. Obviously- later you will see, she did not win with the
55 t -shirt book.
It actually was humorous. Cher said when she prints it
professionally each saying will be a comical style drawing. Like
an interesting character wearing the shirt. She's trying to match
up stereotypes to make it funny. Here's the 55 t-shirts that hit
many genres:

1. I admit I am vain
2. Looks aren't everything
3. Believe
4.Invest in yourself
5. Why?
6. Look at my eyes when you talk to me
7.I love manly men
8.Love Life

9.Smile it doesn't Hurt
10.Plant a tree
11. Thank the Troops. Again and again and again.
12. Royal pain in the ass
13. 5 Pick- up lines that suck:

I'm really single now.
What did you say your name was?
Did we meet before?
How old are you?
Is that a wedding ring?

14. My Boss is not cool
15.Show some love
16. Pssst....I know you are checking me out
17. Lickity split
18.Queer eye for the right guy
19. I prefer ladies
20. I prefer men
21. I'm undecided
22 .Look closer. I 'm almost perfect
23.If you don't have something nice to say- say it to the person
next to me.
24. Spread it- happiness that is.
25. Soldiers Kick ass
26.I work hard appreciate me
27. Money isn't everything- most of the time
28. I'm the boss till my kids get home
29.Respect your elders
30. Hotties who read this can approach
31. Bare all
32. Lazy people apply for welfare
33.Single & desirable
34. Liars can suck it
35. I am the proud sponsor of ME
36. Yes, I am single and I don't have any baggage

37. Yes, I am single and I do have baggage
38.Prejudicepeople- need not apply
39. Queen of the dipshits
40. King of the dipshits
41. I am man here me complain
42.I a woman hear me complain
43 .I am child –help me escape
44. It is true- many good looking people don't get approached because you think I am already taken. Take a chance!
45. Where am I?
46. Rain or shine I'm good.
47. I am in La la land
48. Who owns me?
49. Just say "hi"
50. I bite
51. My eyes are red. I did just smoke.
52. Stop wondering and ask
53.my mom said I'm special
54. Fu**K . Yes. I am wearing this shirt so your kids can read it.
55. I bought a book of T-shirt sayings

Sonny: Okay I guess I have to take it with me and look it over since you went and printed it! Loser!
Cher: That's a good for a shirt!

Sonny: Ugghh.
Sonny: Hey listen, I wrote something and I was thinking of writing a bigger story out of it. Let me know what you think. I brought it with me:
It's really rough -so bear with -as I read it. I know I always say it's a work in progress... but…

It's fiction. These scientist found out that the psychics are not crazy people. But the government won't let the scientists get that out, unless it's for government purposes.

Cher: Obviously. Continue please.

Sonny: The government secretly uses intuitives and psychics for research and gain knowledge from enemies that normal people don't have access to get.

These scientists realized that most people only use 3% of their brains on a day to day basis- which psychics use about 40% of their brain on the left and right side. That is why they are highly communicative and have this intelligence to reach other dimensions of existence.

The government through these studies started with psychics found that they cannot clone these gifts. They were trying to clone people and they *did* succeed- but could *not* clone the energy of the soul of the people or their intuitive gifts. The government goes on to sell the public lies. Specifically those abilities of psychics are just television scams and a farce- like most television shows- all acts. Reality shows are the farthest from reality. It's a joke. And people believe it all.

They do this because they want all the good psychics with abilities to work for them only. The part that the government is unaware of – is the fact that the psychics are highly intelligent and most of them are considered empaths- they can sense and feel from other people.

This means the psychics know the government's true motives and now the psychics take advantage of the governments dishonestly and turn it on them. The psychics do only what is for the greater good of people- anything other than goodness they can manipulate to make the government think otherwise.

All the experimenting the government does with drugs and farming and cloning- the psychics try to fix their errors but some things become irreversible.

72

These telepathic people have mind meetings across the world. Some call these telepathic people *aliens* even though they look normal and regular. But aliens are anything foreign - that's the definition of alien- so all of us are alien if you really want to look at it- Anything foreign. The real question is foreign from *where*?

The telepathic mind communicators decide to become *inaccurate*. The psychics also agree to do the same for the government officials. They *fawk* the government.
That's all I got so far.

Cher: Its good- but there probably a lot of stuff like that out there.
Sonny: Really. You think so?
Cher: Yeah.

Sonny: There a lot of things. But I guess they are more sci-fi. It depends if I try to tie in real life stuff- or if I keep it really out there with the characters I create.
Cher: Yeah you could totally do that.

Sonny: Maybe I will keep as a short. Then it can make the reader think however they want. *Or* I could have multiple endings…
Cher: Yeah- I like all the others stuff better- you know the TV shows are great- those are ones to beat. Maybe stick to doing those things more and put less pressure on yourself to do fiction in a big way.

Sonny: I see you what you are doing! You Bitch! You want me to forget about the writing contest so *You* can win the fifty grand! You forget. I know you too well!
Cher: Awe. Snap again. You caught me.

Sonny: Sarcastic dog! You are so competitive! Where do you get that from? Your mom? Or dad?

Cher: Honestly- I don't know where I get it from. But you sure as hell bring it out in me!

 Sonny: Did you ever think about how some people are such freaking assholes and others can be nice no matter what?

Cher: I never really took the time to-but -Maybe shit happened to that asshole.

 Where did this subject come from? It's like your brain switches and then another subject comes in-

Sonny: Well what I think – I am saying is that maybe we are all the same at the beginning. Then the effects of the world set-in and we get "ruined" by experiences- but we also get better because of those experience. You know like some bad shit – then good shit happens too. This makes us be able to call each other out on stuff-

Cher: I know what you are trying to verbalize. Yes. *Shit happens*. Where did I hear that before? Is that a book by Wayne Dyer?

Sonny: What? Are you listening to me?

Yes, I mean, *No*. The book name is "*Shift Happens* "by Wayne Dyer!

 You are a moron. Now back to what I was saying…but it can make a dull personality. Null. Blah. Cabesh?

Cher: Yep.

Sonny: How do you know what true happiness feels like anyway?

 Am I just happy if I say I am happy?

Cher: It's just a word to describe.

Sonny: You mean a word to describe a feeling?

Cher: That could be stress again! Hahahha.

Sonny: I believe true happiness is something that may not be tangible- there's good and evil in our world right? But if that balances... how come I always yearn for something that is fulfilling- something I feel I have to accomplish. It's on-going with me.

Cher: Maybe it's because we both have voids. We don't have relationships other than friends. That could be why.
 Maybe if we had *more*- we *would* feel content.
Sonny: Maybe. I know with work I always feel like I need to do more- be more and have larger goals.
But that I feel is a good way to be.

 Cher: Yes, I feel the same- but when it is okay that we reach the goals and feel that fulfillment – like saying - I'm good today I don't have to go out of my way to get that particular thing done. I just want to sit outside and watch the birds on the trees.

Sonny: I don't know. I'm definitely not there yet.
Cher: Maybe if we have boyfriends we would watch the birds on the trees with them and they would slow us down.

Sonny: Priorities and the perception of the priorities. That's the change. That's the real switch.
Cher: Yeah. Maybe.

Sonny: Let's eat. We are getting way to philosophical for our age.

 Sonny: People are going to think we are stoned.
Cher: Totally. That was fer sure a stoner conversation! Are you wearing a t- shirt that says "I 'm an over thinker" or "I smoke the green?"

Sonny: Girl- you are nuts.

The ladies had another conversation after that philosophical spew. They talked about super stars and music legends and how they could- if they wanted – to get them to sleep with them and make a video tape of it. This all came about when Cher brought up Kim Kardashian's new perfume.

Both decided to call it a night. Sonny had to meet a co-worker at 8am in the morning for the next Frommerz restaurant review. Sonny's boss always wanted to check-in on her work and prep her for the next place on the line-up. It was a good work relationship for Sonny. She was responsible and always did well in all the work she did for her bosses.

Cher had to work in the office in the morning- she had to take a ride to Fort Lauderdale to the main office and check-in and drop a few articles. Cher finished an article on the musician Dave Navarro. She was hoping to meet him in person- but that didn't happen. She had to use previous information from interviews he had in the past. Cher said that's how many articles are written when they can't get in to see a star. Cher wrote that he was a Hot Eddie Munster- she said if there was a cartoon show like the Simpsons or family guy- Dave would be perfect!

It's hard for me to believe this young lady writes about such silly things at times- but it is entertaining to others I am sure of that.

Friday afternoon

Friday afternoon both ladies were done working by 2pm. Sonny and Cher texted each other and headed over to meet at a new coffee bar. It wasn't the one that was located close to the order by number restaurant, but near the old Miami hotel. It was the art district. There were lots of cool shops and architecture. Most of Miami was deco looking but over time things changed there as all places do.

The place was called Me-ami Coffee house. Cher and Sonny met there to toss some ideas around and get input from each other.

The sat near an old couple that looked like they were 99 years old. Both with leather skin from over sunbathing. They were happy and looked content in their conversations about grandchildren and the expense of the two coffee lattes they bought.

Cher noticed a handsome man that caused quite a stir at the coffee counter. He was visiting his ex- girlfriend at the counter. She looked like she was 18 and he in his thirties. That was the normal in south Florida. When he approached the counter area to talk to her she turned her back and snubbed him. She pretended he wasn't there and helped the next person in line. His head was steaming- he yelled in a grouchy tone accusing her of sleeping with his roommate- or ex roommate as it sounded. Cher said he made a fool of himself but she still wanted to grab him and kiss him! She said she could mend his broken heart-until Sonny opened her mouth and said :
Sonny: Cher!- I'll give you 5o dollars if you go up to that guy and kiss him in front of that jailbait!

Cher looked at Sonny as if she wanted to fly across the bar and do it! However, by the grace of gods, the man stormed out calling his ex-girlfriend a whore for hire.
That was a blessing for Cher.

Sonny: Too late. Dang! I wanted to see a soap opera today!
 Cher: Pay up.

Sonny: You didn't kiss him! I'm not paying you!
 Cher: You should- for working me like that. Now get me a refill Chia latte, no sugar!
Sonny: Let's just calm down and get back to relaxing like this older couple is doing.

Sonny and Cher looked over at the older couple and they were kissing with tongue! They both described this view as TMITV-

Too Much Information To View. Cher then posted it on Facebook, then on TWITTER.

Sonny got up from her seat and stood in line to purchase another Chi latte and one for Cher. They wanted to stay awhile, it was Friday afternoon and the freaky people were coming out. Both of them loved to people watch. That is where they say they get their best material for writing. It seemed to me they both had enough material coming from themselves and more than they needed in a lifetime!

Sonny brought the latte over to Cher and smiles with an evil smirk.

Cher: Did you put sugar in my latte?
Sonny: Come on – would I do that?

Sonny grinned and sat down as nothing was up. Sonny did put sugar in one of the lattes, but since both ordered the same one with sugar one without. Of course she loved to mess with Cher and gave her the sugar latte. She wanted her to take a sip to get her all roweled -up.

Cher: There is sugar in this!

Sonny switched the cups quickly and said:

Sonny: *Cher*- I was just teasing, here's yours. That was mine. They just got mixed up.
Cher: Ughhh.

A few minutes later it was if it never happened, they were joking around got their notebooks out. They wanted to share some more ideas:

Cher: Hey- last night after dinner, I was inspired to start something really cool. It's something I can't do alone. I would need you to join me. It's a project that we can also make money with if you are game.

Sonny: Share.

Cher: Okay I want to create an online and tangible national publication called "The Evolution *Soul*tion." I also like that name for a book. Maybe I will use it for both a book and a community news publication. Do you get the play on the word soul-ution?

This would include all businesses such as: Restaurants, Mindful Centers, juice bars, and healthy places. Yoga, also services that are health conscious. For an example like pest control that is green without toxic chemicals. Over all it will let consumers know where to go for these services.

Since you recycle and are a green girl, we could start a YouTube series show of episodes of you going to different places. You can be your silly self and talk about being green and ways to help the Earth.
But the epic part is -we mainly have you go into restaurants- since that's your forte' and order the green plate they have available. Ya know something organic. This educates people that maybe there is a restaurant in their neighborhood that is not organic- but they added one organic dish to bring health conscious people in.

 My goal can show that it is worth all restaurants to have at least a few dishes organic. Then the concept will grow and so on and so on and so on!!! It will be global- or national at least. See many restaurants do have one plate organic and if not it will make it popular for them to do it. On top of that happening- big chains will do it as well. Then the BIG picture is that organic farmers and suppliers will grow and more and more healthiness is happening for the earth as a whole! We can make it super fun! You can rate the organic dish you eat and write your review in our publication and feature the best of the best!

Sonny: You are saying we would eat for Free more than now? We'd be two fat Green chicks- the evolution of overeating!
Cher: Come on be serious.

Sonny: I do like the idea. It would be super fun. I am definitely into the name you chose. "Evolution Soultion" It really feels like it's a winner. Plus it is the purpose behind the concept. Awareness, educate and organic growth.
Cher: ARE you in?

Sonny: Sure let's try it and get all the logistics together and see how much time and effort and money it would be.
Cher: Money? Oh my friend-0 we will get sponsors easy. No money needed. I will work on that.

Sonny: Speaking of ideas- this one I have is going to knock you out of the atmosphere. Are you ready?
Cher: Hit me.

Sonny: This is a game show idea. After hearing the other one – another new idea was born- I know this is usually your department- but I had this pop into my head after a meditation. Let me clear my voice…ehhhem. Okay don't laugh at the funny voice I am trying to make. I'll tell you after who I am impersonating if you can't guess it.
Sonny: Oh Boy. Okay. Go for it.

Cher: I'm teaching you all how to cook today. My show features a psychic medium that channels a famous chef. I am using their voice at the moment.

Sonny: Wow! Your voice is really irritating me. Hahahha. Can you turn your *own* voice back on now? *Please.*

80

Cher: Not until you guess who I am trying to be.

Sonny: Let me guess. Chef Ramsy?
Cher: No.
Sonny: I dunno! Tell me. Come on people are looking at us. I going to call Dev over and embarrass you if you don't stop that voice!

Sonny: Okay, okay. It *is Julia Child!*

Cher: Oh Snap! Why didn't I get that! Let me think…
Oh yeah- because *you* didn't sound anything like her!

Sonny: Whateva.

Cher: Great show. Right?

Sonny: I have to say I like this idea better than mine.
Cher: Really? That's a first.

Sonny: Don't get cocky.
Cher: Can we write it up and send it to that producer friend of a friend knows?

Sonny: Sure let's give it a try. Hopefully they won't steal the idea- since we both know that happens a lot.
Cher: Yes. It's far too familiar.

Sonny: I'll write it up and copyright it as entertainment.

Cher: Cool. I'm excited about this one and the psychic judge show.
Sonny: Just imagine if we get our teacher, she's a psychic medium. If we get her on one of our shows! That would be freakin large.

Cher: Seriously? I don't think she would do that kind of show. I mean the Julia Childs one. I can see her agreeing to the Psychic judge panel. That would be cool!

Sonny: Yeah you're right on that. Maybe we can suggest to the producers that they get Lisa Williams for the channeling Julia Childs!

Cher: *That* -I can see. Is that her name Lisa Williams? Or are we mixing her up with that other lady on TV the New York medium lady? Any hoo- picture Lisa or whoever on the set of the show, with that unique voice. Calling in the spirit of Julia Childs- then creating a yummy dish she cooked did in the past- giving the audience cooling advice and direction as she has the same movements and personality as the *original* Julia Childs.

Sonny: How do you know Julia Childs anyways? She's like ancient.
Cher: Dudette. Really? I am in the restaurateur world – we know all popular chefs throughout time!
Sonny: No comment. I plead the 5th amend.

Cher: Maybe I can Channel Julia Childs. I can learn from our teacher!
Sonny: I think that is really a super duper-incredibly bad idea. Did I stress that enough?

Cher: Why? Our teacher literally said that everyone has the ability to connect.
Sonny: And…

Cher: With permission.
Sonny: Leave it to the seasoned.

Cher: Did you mean seasoned as in experienced or seasoned as in spicy!
Sonny: The play on the word was not on purpose. Leave it to

ANYONE else other than you- is my point.

Cher: Whatever.
Sonny: Get it set and lets' move on the ideas.

Cher: Will do. Pronto

> **Sonny:** Well- I have something new to share. I know you would never think that I would write this style but-- I wrote two children's books! I wrote them for that lady that pays me to be a ghost writer. They are easy to read and are for kids 5-7years old. This first one teaches them how to research things they are interested in learning. Carol the lady I told you about that I write for she's having an artists do the cartoon pictures to match I the words. It is in the rough till I get it finished.
>
> **Cher:** who knew?
> **Sonny:** Okay just check this book out:

It's called: Planes, Trains and Golf shoes.

 Cher: Just give them to me I can read them later. I don't want you to read me a kid's book here. They already look at us like freaks.
Sonny: Awe- come on.
 Cher: Just hand them over- I will look through them *now*, since you are giving me puppy dog eyes.

Cher: I like it. Its good and you can make it really interactive. You can put some space in the back of the book for them to draw a train or color something. I am very surprised. You did well. Kudos!

Sonny: Thank you very much! I really love this other one better. It's a story about a boy who passed on and he still is remembered as a bright light.
Cher: Do you have it with you? Let me read it.

Sonny: Yep. Okay. I didn't want to do all kiddie talk tonight! Hahaha.
Cher: No seriously. Read it. It makes me feel like a kid again.

Sonny: This one is called: The enchanted boy.
This is a story of a special boy who's nick- name was Sugar RTZ. He was such an inspiration to others; they gave him the additional   name "The Enchanted boy."

They called him "Sugar RTZ" because he was sweet, fast and fit. He was an artistic master.
He made a positive difference in so many lives.

He was a teacher, a friend and skillful mentor to many who crossed his path.

"Sugar RTZ" was a teacher with wisdom and skills… passing this information on to others, to make a better place for all.

He didn't realize it, at the time, but he had this **light** around him that made him so special. Some called this **"light"** his incredible **positive Energy**.

Humble at times…he was always **Loving** and **kind**.

He beamed of **humor** and quick wit… when he joked the **joy** he let out was tremendous… to some he made their stomachs hurt with the laughter!

His presence was known…Once you saw him you had to **smile.**

His **smile** was like a bolt of lightning... it hit you and made you feel **electric**

Young children looked up to him for he was their **gallant knight**.

He walked with a slight bounce and a glimmer in his brown eyes…

Everyone who saw him felt the **charge** of his **immense energy**

Throughout his life he walked this earth,

Helping and **teaching** others **meaningful skills.**

He taught **skills** that would help each and every one of them **grow** towards their **goals the future.**

His **charismatic charm** was only in the **purest** form.

He knew **right** from wrong and was **strong** from knowing it.

Alas… When it was his time to pass… he still brought **sunshine** on all who knew him.

Today he still **lives** in **minds** of many, and spreads his **love** and **charm**. The lucky will always **enjoy** his **celestial presence.** "Sugar RTZ" is the Enchanted Boy, that we all see as a **shining star.**

Cher: That's one is good. I like the name too. That can be a book parents give to their kids when they ask: Mommy where do we go when we die?"

Multi-talented

These ladies really had some killer ideas. It was like their brains never stopped working. They had a mission to do as much as they could; unfortunately they were just filling voids most of the time.
Between the both of them- they must have had hundreds of money making ideas. It only takes one to make it big. But the

ladies didn't have long term focus, as of now anyway. I do have to hand it to them; they were hard workers. They did the workload of ten people in my opinion.

Since they started meditating they had gotten more and more clear ideas. It gave them better focus. I am sure that over a few months of meditating it will gear them in the perfect direction.

That Friday they stayed at the coffee shop from 2pm until 7. They had another coffee date at the place near the restaurant. They both headed over in Cher's car.

Friday *night* coffee date
Friday night and the coffee date begins… I believe it was Sonny's date that had an extreme impact on both ladies.
For some reason this man will remain nameless. He was the coffee date. He was insanely gorgeous. He was described to me as looking as like a young Van Dame. Cher and Sonny most likely have no clue who that is, but it fit the description- and that's what I imagined. He's physique was solid muscle – features on his face flawless- beyond good looking- he was outright the bomb!

There were great things about to happen on this Friday night…but was it a *Lesson* or just a happening of life?

Back to my point- he was someone they thought had a wonderful aura- great energy- until they realized his energy wasn't looking for a date with a woman! The ladies told me- when another man walked by the table during the date-this Van Damme look alike would stop talking to Sonny and stare at all the gentlemen's asses while passing the table.

It was comical in the sense that at one point both Sonny and her Muscle date stopped and did a total head turn on a hot male. It was a guy that looked just like Adam Lambert from American Idol! Cher was on the sideline watching the auras for their bet.

86

She too, stopped to stare at him. It was totally obvious the muscle man was on the other side of the team.
It was hilarious. Cher told me she was in love with Adam Lambert because he looked like young Elvis. I would certainly agree. He was my favorite on American Idol that season.

Well this situation at the coffee bar gets better. As the Cher about 2 tables to the left and Sonny up close-both tried to read muscle man's aura *and* Adam-Elvis's aura! Sonny and Cher claimed they both visually saw an energy connection. They described it as looking like an orange light as a string that connected from one man to the other!
I guess there was a match made that night! That was when Sonny decided to get up and say Hello to her friend a few tables down as she excused herself from the date. Meanwhile, the Adam look alike swooped in and sat in her chair next to muscle man. They started talking and looked like they were exchanging digits- so Sonny walked up and asked him if he was cool with her taking off with her friend! All was working out for the men anyway!

Sonny and Cher held in their laughs as they walked outside to really let it out. Sonny wasn't mad, she thought it was hilarious. She was bummed that she could've had a new shopping pal . She kept the notion that maybe he would call her for that and she would win the $60! Cher said for her not to hold her breath and put her palms out to get the cash that night!

The ladies didn't speak other than texting-for the next few days they were busy with other obligations and assignments. They would meet on their usual Thursday for dinner next week.

One text Cher sent Sonny was:
Meat any New Men 4 Me?
I waz hoping u cld set me up with a shunk

Sonny texted back:
UR not FunE
Meat u 4 cofe or food @6

Cher - with her bad texting meant a shunk is half hunk and half female qualities. She was trying to be funny. *Trying* I emphasize.

Dinner Number 5 Cinco

Thursday 6pm -They both ordered the same pasta dish and had great sarcastic conversations. For their 5th dinner-same place - same time as usual. It was time for the two writers to chat and share about their newfound fav place for intelligence. This was talking about Mindful Center and of course her new abilities.

This night was a bit different than the last few. Sonny felt the need to share her dreams. She claimed her dreams were more vivid than ever. She was sharing the ones she wrote with Cher at dinners but she swears ever since she started meditating every night with the energy art she bought- she sees and remembers more. Since she saw that energy art the psychic teacher called a channeled mandala. Sonny said her dreams gave her messages.

Cher was in awe since she had some of the same experiences. Both had detailed dreams that she too can remember in her waking state of mind. Both decided to write down what they were dreaming and see if any of it was good material for their freelance writing. As of last week they were happy with all the insights they received- still they were wanting more.

Cher still needed some information about astral travel and later that night when at the healing center asked the psychic teacher to explain what and how to experience it. Sonny and Cher got there early so they could ask her a few questions before the manifesting class. They were told that there was a mandala specifically for helping people astral travel, but they would have to use a Smokey quartz crystal placed on top of this mandala art- for safety reasons. That was the turning point for the girls. They loved the "safety" feature- it made it so much more enticing to them to have the unknown tied in with a touch of danger.

 The psychic teacher explained that it wasn't a danger of getting hurt, but seeing and sensing occurrences or visions from a place they may or may not want to be or see- they possibly could see or visit a negative occurrence. This is why she explained that using the safety crystal would bring only positive surroundings and feelings. She explained it would keep their minds from traveling in a low frequency place basically a dimension other than earth dimension.

They sat and chatted at the restaurant:

Sonny: Hey girl... how was your week?
 Cher: Mine was good.

Sonny: That's *all*- good?
 My week was epic! I had so many killer dreams- I have so much material for my short s book that I might have to write another volume!

Cher: I had some really weird dreams but I didn't get up to write them down. I guess I was lazy.

Sonny: I gotta read you this new one. This dream was so detailed I thought it was really happening. I woke up with tears in my eyes and sniffling!

Cher: That doesn't sound epic in a good way-

Sonny: I was at some sort of big place where it had escalators, but not like a mall or anything like that. I was there to meet with this man that was going to help me with a painting I had with me. The painting was like 8x11 in size and had blues and whites and yellow on it was special in some way. I originally met with him not knowing who he was- when he showed up – he was with another guy. Both were there to see about helping me.

I showed them the painting and they were talking about bringing it to another person and that it was indeed very unique. All of us- me and the men parted. Later that day in that same area The first guy that I met with the painting was playing tennis- I was also there to play tennis. At that point we were playing against each other in a fun way. By the way this guy looked like that guy Michael from the TV series Burn Notice – and No- I wasn't Fiona.
Okay back to me- I was playing tennis with him, we were laughing- so much fun. After the game, we hung out- it felt like years we knew each other although we were in that same place with the escalators.

Then in a split second he looked into my eyes and said" I really want children." I looked into his beautiful handsome face and said I always wanted children too." He then looked at me like- yeah right. That was the impression I got from his facial expressions. I at that exact second realized I was 44 years old. That was why I got the "look" from burn notice guy! I didn't have a mirror- he didn't say it to me- I just knew it. He walked away and I knew he loved me and I loved him. I started to tear up as I walked away from him and went upward on an elevator.

I felt so hurt and upset and I kept repeating to myself- I really wanted kids, I really wanted kids, he was perfect for me." I approached the top of the escalator platform to the next floor.

My Father was standing there. He was looking at me and saw my tears. He hugged me and said he loves me and it's time to move on. I walked away feeling better, but I was crying. I woke up – and felted Burned! Thanks Michael Weston! Sarcasm and more sarcasm to the max!

Cher: Ha! I love it! I love that guy Michael Weston. You totally got burned in your dream by him. I love that strange connection. How weird was it that you were 44 years old. I wonder if we ask our psychic teacher if the numbers mean anything. Ya know like numerology?

Sonny: I don't know but I woke up like I must have been crying a long time in that dream. At the end I felt like I walked miles. My legs were fatigued when I got out of bed.

Cher: Maybe it was all the tennis you played in the dream- Sarcasm city! HA... got ya!

Sonny: Oh my friend you are extremely hilarious- you must be hanging around with all the Californian comedians-not.

Sonny: You're a bitch- you gotta admit that your dream was ridiculous. But I will give you kudos on writing it as a short. It was entertaining. I thought there was going to be more on the painting and it was going to be a mystery thing. Then you up and changed the vision of it to tennis! Kudos-my friend.

Cher: It's our 5th anniversary! Just a one more time eating our pasta dinners and we will be on the next assignment of tapas from Tapa world on 6th street.

Sonny: Stop saying that so loud. Dev is going to think we really are a couple!

Cher: We are we are Sonny and Cher.

Sonny: Ha. Ha.

Cher: Here's Dev.
Sonny: Hi Dev- You know it send us our regular!

Dev: Sure ladies, nice to see you. I'll put the order in. I'll be back with your drinks.
Sonny: I love when he smiles at me.

Cher: At you? Really?
Sonny: That's okay you can have him. I'm on a hunt for Michael Weston.

Cher: so what would you want in a man? What did you write as your manifest for a good match?
Sonny: I am and allow myself to meet a man that respects me and I him, he attracted to me and I to him. He has good work ethic and treats me and everyone nicely. He can be young but not too young. He doesn't mind catering to my needs and makes me feel valuable. He is a business owner and is honest. He is monogamous to me and I to him. We meet this month of February and we meet in an unconventional way.

Cher: Wow, you really did listen to psych- teach. You said it verbatim of how she told us. I am impressed with you.
Sonny: that's right. What's yours?

Cher: Okay I am and I allow myself to meet a man that is polite and kind, he can cook and is bright. He is attracted to me and I to him. We have common interests. He treats me with respect and I to him. We trust each other and I want him to be tall and medium build and has a funny sense of humor. I want my guy to be a business owner too. That was a good one you said. Oh yeah I want my man to be a few years older than me age 30 to 35 is cool.

Sonny: Nice. Okay. He sounds good. I approve.
Cher: yeah. Where we gonna meet them. I am sick of the coffee house and bars seem to have the stragglers- the ones that have no respect and always look for chick that will sleep with them in the same night. Dogs shits.

Sonny: Well, maybe when we get our psychic reading next week we can ask where we can meet good men!

Sonny: I have another dream to share if you want to hear it.

Cher: I don't know why you always ask me- you know I love this!

Sonny: This was a dream too, but a different night. No tears' promise.
Cher: Go on-

Sonny: I had a dream that I was standing and felt a web or small spider on my hands, I tried to wipe the webs away and knew I was bitten by small spiders , then I felt a spider on my lower part of my backside. There was a person there not sure who, I couldn't sense or see a face, but they said wow, there is a spider on my back just as I had thought I did, they took their hand and picked it off my back and tossed it quickly away, I didn't see it but I imagined it to be black and a good size 3 inches or so big, and black. The person that took the spider off said it was a Siberian or something of that nature, at this time I knew that I was just bitten or as I sensed that my base of my spine is being recharged as a spiral of energy moved within me- I also realized my hand could feel the webs and small spiders. All of this has activated my hands for healing once again. I felt like I had done this before. Maybe it was another life or something. But that night -before I slept, I asked the angels and spirit guides to please help heal me so that I can help heal others in need. I know that they heard me.

Cher: Whoa- that was crazy! Do you think all the trips of us learning all this energy healing and parallels and energy exchanges are doing this to you?

Sonny: Yeah, most certainly. But I talked to my mother last week and she told me that we had some intuitive people in our family tree- and Indian healers too.

I think it's similar to my dream and also goes in line with what our psychic teacher is saying- we all have this energy in us- and when we allow it to come out or activate it- it's there. I guess it's getting stronger because I want it to be strong. I also want to learn more and more.

Cher: Yeah- I know I feel a difference since we have started meditating. It's good. It is a peaceful feeling and I continue to be brilliant a t my work at the same time!

Sonny: You're so vain!

Cher: Am I? Or am I honest.

Sonny: You are vain. But truthful.

Cher: I love this food here. It's just always the same! Hahahha...

Sonny: I know. Don't they ever change the variety?

Cher: Hahahha. We could get something different but then you'd get fired and I wouldn't be able to eat for free every Thursday night!

Sonny: Yes. My job is mint- I never want to give this up!

Both girls finished their meals. They had the usual same small talk with Dev the waiter then got their check. Dev finally asked the girls what their names were. Sonny said her name was Dee and Cher said hers was Lori.

Afterwards they drove to the Mindful center for their 8pm class. This night is was about clearing energy and being a clean channel of energy. The psychic teacher talked a lot about respect of others and how healing requires focus and intention of love and goodness. Both Sonny and Cher looked into each other's eyes when their teacher mentioned "respect of others."

She gave them this handout in hopes they would read it.
Be a CLEAN, CLEAR CHANNEL

What does this mean?
This is part of keeping you and your energy pure. Being a clean and clear human is good for you and others around you. Whether you are being clean with foods you eat or from staying clear from negative thoughts, you can keep the mind and body clear as a conduit of light. A clean clear channel is common courtesy.
It means you will not perform and energy healing on anyone if you are in an altered state of mind: which includes: alcohol, marijuana or any mind altering drugs. Even one drink can disturb the energy flow and disrupt it in a negative way.

To practice energy healing you can learn to help others heal themselves. But first you must be a clean clear channel.
Would you want someone practicing on you while they were drunk or high?
When the mind is altered the INTENT is not true, lowering the vibrational energy that comes from you or surrounds you of which is NOT Pure Light.
You could possibly be bringing this low vibration energy into another person unknowingly and is very disrespectful. I can give another example that maybe you would never think of as

95

distorting energy: What about watching a horror movie then performing reiki or energy healing on another person? That too is a form of unclear energy, anything that alters your mind to an unhealthy state. A thought has energy. This energy can be low vibration or high vibration. Keep it clean and clear. Keep it positive.

If you choose to alter your mind, which I suggest not, especially if you plan on performing and energy work which includes psychic readings, reiki or crystal healing keep the negative distorted energy for practicing on yourselves or not at all. Energy healing is about love and light energy with pure loving intent.

During the class

Sonny and Cher made strange faces and pretended they could do no wrong. It's Funny how the universe works-its synchronicity. After class they went to the neighborhood book store to look up more info on astral travel and telepathy. Cher and Sonny both were receiving such a flow of information from their dreams and meditations they wanted to try to automatic write messages from spirits.
 The psychic teacher talked only for a few minutes about how to do it. Sonny said she was going to practice it soon as she got home from the book store that same night.

Sonny told the psychic teacher about her dreams and visions- the teacher told Sonny that she and Cher were mostly likely already channeling information from their spirit guides. Especially because all the dreams she described had some connection to elevated knowledge. Basically, it was stuff that was very different than Sonny's personality and words she may not regularly use.

Sonny went home and got a pen and notebook without lines on it. She sat and asked her friend Ginny Riggs that had passed into the light at age 15- to speak to her through auto-writing. Within a few minutes Sonny felt that someone had taken her hand and guided her to write a message. First the letter W. Then the letter I, then the letter N. It spelled WIN.

Then her hand automatically wrote G then R. These were the initials of her friend!

She was so excited- she couldn't get any more information and possibly lost that connection. Sonny spoke aloud as if the spirit of her friend could hear her voice. She said" I will contact you tomorrow night if that's Okay. Good night. I love you and I will win. I am a WINNER!" Sonny felt amazed at her and what occurred. She got her shower then went to bed.

Cher decided to channel. She sat with her notepad and asked for a "spirit of knowledge." One that could give her insight. Cher was still in her room and suddenly she heard a voice. She lived alone. This voice seemed to be from the angelic realm- as Cher described. She claimed she felt *his* energy. She believed it was a male. She heard words and wrote them as fast as she could hear them. She started to hear them so fast that she barley could keep up writing them down.

Cher clairaudiently heard :
"We begin with consciousness-everyone needs to have the intuition realized here and now to know what can be accomplished by our goals and standards needed in all the realms. Complete consciousness doesn't help all to get higher knowledge we must work together as a team in such groups to do so. Feel the loving energy of those who like to learn and

involve themselves in this environment.

This alone can change the world on a better higher level. Do what you can and encourage others to do so as much as they can since they too can utilize all the skills they are gifted and become one with everyone. Gifts that can enhance us all to be unique loving entities of the spheres and to the continue life as better loving environment to prove who we are and what we can become and will endure love throughout megathons of worlds not divided by hate and destruction on earth.

This can be abolished simply by manmade bombs and taken away in a flash. Stop this and make it loving not fighting money and hurting it is not needed and should have been stopped a long time ago in my opinion. Do what you can I conclude this discussion. Love and life to you and yours who appreciate the good in all living things through all universes. She hears the name *Ma Ho Chan*-

Cher was floored that she heard a *voice and* auto-wrote that message- it was real! She communicated and it was beautiful. She thanked the spirit and asked him to help her as needed in the future.

Cher was grateful that she connected to a guide – she was humbled and stayed up later in that night to write a message to herself and the universe:

"Sometimes I think about all the things I am grateful for in life. Family – I want to name each one- including those that are not present on earth; I thank the air, the earth, the plants animals and even bugs. I thought of a palmetto bug- they scare me and I don't want them in my home. Some people believe they are the worse living creatures ever. I admit they aren't pretty to look at and I scream and jump when I come across one- Then I think of what they do. To me I see they just exist. They don't put chemicals on everything, they don't take pharmaceuticals that get washed out of people's bodies and go into the water system, and they don't create things that give negative vibrations that cause cancer. They don't inject our food with unknowns or hormones.

They don't try to clone everything and feed us GMOs. We do that- people do. We create trash and we trash our planet. We do that. I want to help the palmetto bug get outside of my house safely and should be the one that wants to crush me! I am thankful to live on this beautiful earth and now I am being taught and trained to live more like a palmetto bug rather than a human always commented that humans are the bugs of the earth and I was one of them.

They are better than us- better than humans- I am thankful for realizing this. Although I am a hypocrite in this life, but in reality - I can make reasonable changes that help save the human name. I am not an extremist- I am an extreme thinker- I need to learn action. I need to fulfill my commitments 100% in a positive way."

Cher put down her notepad and fell asleep happy and proud in her bed.

Cher had been working hard on writing projects and had to finish an article for the magazine by Tuesday. So she needed to sleep to be productive. Part of her wanted to stay up all night and listen to the spirit that brought her the message.

Sonny's dream and message

The next day Sonny woke up and felt she had a dream- she also felt she went to another time- she said it was like she was someone else. Basically viewing someone else's life occurrence, it was very detailed.

This is what Sonny experienced and described of her vision:

This woman was on her way to being a "stand in" in a movie in Miami, it was 7am in the morning, it had just started to rain, and the roads had gotten slick.

I – felt I was her or viewing her –
I was driving a Jeep wrangler/soft top and half doors. I was moving into the overpass lane and then quickly decided not to. The moment I looked over and a big ass gas truck was near the jeep I was driving- The truck was at top speed. *BAM!*
My jeep spun out from the left side of the road over 4 lanes- then to a full 360 degree spin. It was like I was in slow motion. I saw like 12 cars coming straight at me. I noticed that I was looking at then the wrong way traffic should be going.

Then I was driving the red jeep- ended across the other side of the four lane highway- on the right side of the road- and *smash* hitting the cement guard wall with the jeep. I felt as if I had forgot or missed a few minutes after the crash. Suddenly I heard a man saying "Hey, sweetie? Hey can you hear me? Can you move your legs?"

An ambulance was at the location roadside. The man was from the rescue team. I couldn't see his face- everything was super blurry. I felt I was half out of it- the man told me I hit several plastic poles from the overpass divide. They had cracked and come in the back of open jeep. Some poles hit the outer part of the jeep and some flew inside the jeep doors and hit me on the head.

My head had contusions; that's the word the man said to me. I really felt the pain for a moment.

Before all of this happened, I remember just driving and the rain just started to fall. Then I heard a young man's voice.
I heard a voice that said "put your seatbelt on." I heard that at the beginning of the vision, as I was driving in the jeep. This was before the accident. I remembered I was the only one in the jeep.
The vision went back to the scene after the jeep hit the wall. My whole body was in the middle of the jeep. I heard rescuers asking me if I could move my legs because the driver's door was completely smashed inward.

I felt the rescuers take my body out of the jeep and put me in an ambulance. I went to the hospital; I had no broken bones, only cuts and bumps on my head and face. I was told by the doctor that the Jeep was completely totaled. He said I was lucky and if I did not have the seat belt I would've been toast. Well, he didn't use those exact words, but that what I felt from him.

The Angel – the voice I heard to put the seat belt on- I believe- I felt his presence in this situation. I felt he was friend from high school- it sounded familiar- his voice. It was a good friend of mine. I felt like he saved me and visited me in this dream. He was a great friend, hilarious and a surfer dude type. That is what I felt. It felt so real.
I just knew that he had passed in a car accident when we were in high school.

It was not this accident, I saw in the dream- because I know he had unfortunately hit a tree. It was like a vision within my dream. I don't know how to explain it. It was a feeling, not from seeing it visually in this dream. I don't know if it was a dream within a dream.

It was amazing I seriously felt that accident and visually saw the details of this dream or maybe it was an astral travel?

Maybe I had this connection because my friend had passed in high school, I had prayed for him- that he and his family would be happy healthy and safe, where-ever they are.
I believe the benefits are a long lasting friendship between us; he is always in my prayers'.

I have a friend looking out for me. An Angel that was from real life –

I woke up feeling like this accident was me. Like it was my life, and my friend from high school... maybe it was me? Or *maybe* it wasn't – but it surely felt real.

Morning *contact*
Cher finished writing her dream down and got a text from Sonny.

Sonny texted Cher around 9 am, Cher called her shortly after she got the text "cal me Emerg-en -c."

Cher wanted to share all the cool dreams and messages as did Sonny. They actually spoke on the phone and shared instead of texting one another.
Cher was over exaggerating everything ... she wanted to top Sonny's experiences and said that she channeled a spirit that was either Einstein or some other super scientist!

The information she auto-wrote was *clearly* not from her. These were her auto-written notes that she read over the phone to Sonny that morning;

Einstein says...

"There can be frequencies of transference. It is a vibration that is understood by the human. There are vibrancy codes that exist. The soul is simply energy. This energy can hold or release frequencies. These can be positive or negative or neutral in the soul's energy.

  Imagine the soul's energy is a round ball of light. It can be anywhere any dimension any place of existence.
If you have ever looked at a tree trunk that has been cut, whereas you can visually see the rings in the trunk indicating the years of that trees life. This I compare to the soul rings or imprints in the soul energy.
Emotions are vibrations that can be held and stored in a soul's energy.
Only the frequency of a strong intentional thought of the keeper of that soul- can release or hold that energy.

This can be done consciously or subconsciously, due to the fact that all souls can live in one or more dimension simultaneously. This is known in the human language as a parallel life.

Some of you humans call this a past life- but time is no matter to the soul energy- for it exists infinitely. Humans will eventually understand this.

Transferring negative frequencies can happen from one human to another- an example is from a hug/contact.
There can be a thought of a human that is negative frequency. This is a frequency code. That thought/emotion is a frequency code that can be released by another frequency code- also

known to humans as a positive emotion or vibration that releases. I can state this code system as being a high megahertz that is available within humans. Humans have the vibration code and mind skill to emit or transfer this code out of their body into the world. Humans can also do this or receive from outside sources such as sounds that are coded or decoded for the particular purpose- That it is needed or transcended out into the atmosphere.

Many humans believe they "come" to earth preprogrammed with certain destinies. That is a farce. They always can de- code or re- code themselves with frequencies to reach their potentials- with health, emotions and fulfillment.

Understanding the code is the key of a human's life on earth.

Is there an afterlife?
There is no afterlife.
There are parallels.

You are thinking at this moment- that many people *do* have pasts- since many people have had regressions that have been noted by regression professionals on earth.

But what makes them past or a past life...?
The clothing? The surroundings one sees in the experience?

Maybe the "time" you call 2014 is actually earlier than 850 B.C.
You are taught – programmed that that *is* correct information.
Right? Or is it my child?
What labels humans use to "know" what is a *beginning* and that *there is no end.* Infinite, my child. Infinite. I will teach you more."

Sonny: Whoa! That was crazy! What the heck...*you really* think that came from Einstein?

Cher: I guess. It had to come from someone way evolved- scientific- something!
I hope that spirit comes back!

Sonny: Are you sure that wasn't you? I mean, what *if-* that was your higher self fawking with you!!
Cher: What? You are insane.

Sonny: Nat-uhh. Remember in the book the teach sent us? It said stuff about how the energy of you- your all knowing you or higher self can contact us.
Cher: That's too way out there for me to understand.

Sonny: I like it. I'm impressed with *whoever* that was – or *you.*

Why only six dates for the bet?
The ladies decided on six dates because they said twelve would be too many and the number 6 meant healthy relationship.

Who knows- where they read that information from! In reality they chose 6 dates because that was how many days they were eating at that restaurant assignment- and it made it easier for them to meet for dinner and their dates either before or after. The coffee house was actually close in location to the restaurant. It all seemed to work out splendidly according to them.

It was Friday night again-Coffee anyone?

There wasn't a workshop at the Mindful center that night. The psychic teacher must have had a night off. Sonny and Cher had to make other plans. Although the mindful center was their first choice, they drove straight over to the coffee bar to meet two more men instead. Friday nights were really crowded at the coffee shop. There was a teenager playing guitar for tips inside. He was a decent musician for a coffee bar. He didn't sing, he just played a few songs acoustic.

They met their dates by telling them what table they would be sitting –since the tables were numbered at the coffee house. If by chance someone was at the table they agreed to text the dates letting them know what they were wearing instead.

Sonny's had to text her date since someone was at her table that night. Her text to the date said "c-u soon im wearing blu tank ☺."
Each girl found their dates and begun the *process* as they say.

Sonny and Cher became obvious to their suitors that they were reading their dates - one date, up and left after the first 10 minutes of meeting. He thought Sonny had some sort of issue or disorder because she kept looking around his body to read his aura. You have "No couth," he said as he left. She never looked him in the eyes when she talked to him. She was really rude to say the least. He thought she was checking out his "package" and nothing more! That caused her to lose those sixty dollars in a snap!

Cher's date was *not having* her roll her eyes up and down at him either. He got up and called her "a girl that was only looking for material items to sum up his net worth!" He assumed she was looking at his fancy watch and expensive shoes- they were Prada.

Cher laughed as she was on the mission of the aura read and

forgot about the *connecting* for meeting a man for a relationship. Both were caught up in their "game."

These ladies were really acting unruly with the whole reading other peoples energy.

Obviously the ladies left the coffee bar since they got dropped and kicked.

Saturday afternoon

Sonny and Cher went to the Mindful Center that following afternoon. There was a meditation on Saturday at noon. They arrived early to talk to their psychic teacher. They told her about what happened on their coffee dates. Boy, she was angry at them both. She ripped them a new one!

She lectured them on respecting others, and that permission was needed before formally reading others auras. Especially with them using their bad intentions. She was super hard on them. They both thought she didn't want them to come back to the center. But they were wrong.

After the psychic teacher cooled off, she told them it was a good learning experienced and that she trusted them to *never-ever-* disrespect energy or others again. Sonny and Cher both agreed. They felt like 5 year olds getting scolded for eating too much candy.

They stayed a bit longer with their teacher and she talked of how to be a clean clear conduit. She said if they wanted to learn energy healing for others they would have to know this information. They sat through her 30 minute lecture on that subject and then continued home.

Both ladies said they were sorry and apologized to everyone involved in their shenanigans. They did not call all those dates to formally say that, but the psychic teacher told them a way to connect to the person's soul and ask for forgiveness. She told them it was called "soul talking."

The psychic teacher asked for their emails and said she would send them something she wrote about. It was called the Energy Exchange and How to manifest with it. It would explain how energy can be held and how to emit negative. She told them she would send them the book that same night- this way they could do the soul talking correctly and understand it.

Both ladies gave their emails to their psychic teacher and went their separate ways to their apartments.
Cher looked in her email to see if she received the book – it was an hour after the class was over. She couldn't find it. Cher texted Sonny "U git it yet?" she wanted to know if she received the emailed book.

Sonny replied in about 5 seconds "yep – check ur spambx".
Cher looked again in her email spam and it was there. Sonny texted " I'm reading now. CU tomrw."

Cher downloaded and printed it- Cher always likes paper when reading. She said "it feels better to have the words in my hands."
The following day, the ladies emailed me the book in a zip file. It is a phenomenal read. I copied and pasted it below, so you can read it.

The book their psychic teacher wrote and emailed:

"Exchanges of Energy with humans"

Why is this energy exchange so important?
Well, I believe that in the future, telepathic skills of "listening and receiving" will be the only way of communicating to each other. This will be the new way of living, equally with all energies on earth and beyond.

It seems only fair to be happy, loving and kind, because our world can affect their world since we all are in the same atmosphere. If we all are on higher vibration (which means happy) our atmosphere and all that is in it -makes a better place to reside.
Not only having an even or a balanced energy exchange with these other far-way Places or worlds, but our earth would work much better for all of us humans.

Think about it, because as I see it, right now, what we are doing is not an even energy exchange with our own earth obviously enough, it's not working out too well- ya know with global warming , contaminated water, chemically altered food and all that.

I want an even or positive energy exchange with everyone, everything and all existence.

I listened to these "spirit guides of the Light' and wrote their messages. Read these messages of what they shared to teach us. I hope you like them and can realize how much it all makes sense. Like me, you can "listen too." As these spirit guides and Angels explain, *"Every energy exchange counts!"*

"Let Life Flow- Let the Universe guide you in infinite ways of happiness."

EVERYTHING IS "ENERGY"

Everything is energy. You are energy, a tree is energy, and even a rock has incredible energy.
Understanding about energy can help you make sense of how energy healing works and its healing effects on people, things and you.

Our human bodies need to have high vibrational energies within and around us to heal and maintain on all levels. Physical, mentally, emotionally and spiritually as a whole, to balance and keep us feeling well.
Every day in each of our lives we can pick up energies from things, other people and especially from ourselves.

This includes energy of our thoughts, they are energy too! Thoughts are vibrations and also our physical voices are vibrations. Some of your thoughts or verbal words may or may not be of high frequency (positive energy).

Thoughts we create are considered *thought forms*. Thoughts can be positive or negative or null. If your thought is negative, the energy goes out as negative energy, negative means lower vibrations. If that thought is about you and *is negative* we call that a "self –sabotage energy thought form." These can harm when they are a constant in a person's aura, if these negative vibrations are not cleared out of the aura in sensible time.

Knowing and understanding energy with how it works with our bodies (aura) energy fields is something everyone should be schooled about. You will find that monthly maintenance is a healthy alternative method for cleansing the energy in one's body. One method is using a form of *energy healing* to keep our bodies clean and clear. This clarity keeps us aligned and balanced to feel great. There are many types of energy healing modalities that cleanse our bodies. Reiki healing, Hands of light and Light tunnel energy with crystals are just a few examples.

What is cleansing and clearing?
110

Some people need to *release* unwanted energies from their bodies. When someone needs to let -go or clear themselves it means they need to cleanse their electro-magnetic field around their body aka their auric field. This can also indicate a person's body that needs a physical healing. An emotional or mental healing can also be felt in the aura.

What gets in our aura that makes it negative or heavy?

When debris is in our energy field, "space" or aura, that usually means negative emotions or "junk" may be deep within their auric fields and can be multi-dimensional. This is when a person may need a "cord cutting with replacement, or a deeper release. "This is energy terminology. Energy healing is administered energetically for a person who needs to relive themselves from negative vibrations in their auric field. An example is a "cord cutting "this type of energy healing session allows the negative energy to be released instead of imprinting in the soul.

The purpose of this cleansing and clearing is to feel free of "old or stuck energies that can be mental, emotional, physical or spiritual." This releases "you" of that heavy emotional weight or negative thoughts, worries, and patterns that are not good!

"I *CHOOSE* & ALLOW MYSELF TO LIVE HAPPILY.

I AM THE KEEPER OF MY SOUL."

THE ENERGY EXCHANGE

channeled messages from Angels & Spirit guides for you to think about.

P.S. These quoted messages are unedited and written exactly as they were received.

Many of the messages are self-explanatory, but I wanted to give you my take on them. I would also like *you* to interpret them - in your words. We all have different ways of reading and understanding. I believe that is what makes us unique.

"Everything you do will have meaning-purpose."

"Adherently there are many obstacles in life-one is just a stone in a pond- that enjoys the company"

A human is surrounded by many trials in a huge world, but one person's love can make a big positive difference and be heard.

"Energy surrounds everything in a human's life-make it positive"

Everything that exists is energy. All of us are made up of vibrations. Keep em high vibes.

"Energy is simply positive and negative-choose positive

High vibrations= happiness

"Choose the path that says, I am me"

We always have choices in life. Make decisions with "your" energy, don't be something you really are not or not comfortable with.

"When lessons occur, it is more than one that learns, it is an equal energy exchange on levels, that sometimes   one cannot necessarily "see' at that present moment"

They mean we can be blinded with our emotions and not see the real truth, especially because emotions are not plainly visible. We sometimes disregard listening to our emotional energy, we wait until we see physical proof. I also like to compare our understanding to a dirty window, once we understand the concept of something, the window is *very clear* and clean and easy to see through.

"Speak to others kindly as you receive what you place outwardly."

 "Every thought is energy- notice how and what you think- that "thought energy" affects you and others that 'thought energy' is placed upon."

Thoughts are vibrations just like our physical voices.

They are talking about" thought forms." We can send or place energy of our thoughts on other people. This is done simply by thinking something positive or negative and "sending" it their way/into their aura a.k.a. Electromagnetic field around the human body. The other person can absorb this energy of that particular thought in their aura, affecting them on an energetic level.

"It", is not always about "you" There are many ways to "see" situations or feel emotions- look through others eyes as well as your own"

Well, this sure is a great quote for all of us humans!

113

'Wise humans think positively in all situations'
"mindfulness is healthiness"

I always say and post on Facebook that there are Mind-Full people and there are those people that choose Mind-Less acts.

"Understand only you, make decisions for you, you are the one that makes "choices" If you need to make an excuse, you will see your life decisions will reflect."

Amen to that.

"Sometimes a decision, path can be hard, but knowing you always have a choice is freedom a human is born with. Having a "mind" or thought of your own — is your personal power"

True. Although, we must learn to "use" our power in a good way and good timing is something to factor in.

"Share your compassion of being a "giver" show or explain, or guide to give others assistance, direction with empowerment.

"Doing everything for them diminishes their empowerment and is an un-balanced energy exchange for both of you."

114

"Accept help, support, advice or a compliment. Accepting is balanced energy exchange. Accepting is not taking- Realize this and your life will change for the best. The "Intention "of accepting is balanced- positive."

Accepting is not taking. Many of us do have to re-learn this one. (This is a shout to all the over-givers out there- know your boundaries!)

"The Intention of "taking" is unbalanced negative."

I asked these spirit guides, Can I make this a bumper sticker?

"Speak Kindly of others and think beautifully of yourself."
Love thyself.

"Learn to have happy thoughts, experiences; positive energy makes you attractive on all levels."

Extremely true, who wants to be around a complainer or bummer attitude? Not I.

"Begin a new day with trying something different- it can be a new way to open your car door, a new kind of tea or coffee, or say hello to 5 people before you go to lunch- change monotony."

Live outside your genie bottle. Enjoy life; it's full of fun surprises.

"Be – 'Aware' that Life is well and all around you —see the light and well-ness."

<u>Meaning of Life</u>

L- Learn

I-Identify

F-Find

E- Experience

I interpret this as: learn as much as you can. Experiences lead us to self-discovery. Empowering oneself. Identify life around you with as much clarity as you can. Find new ways to savor and appreciate your life.

EARTH MOONS SHIFTS- meditation with YOU

This is a self-meditation for clearing our own soul's energy; since we are all made of energy and everything in the world is energy- making equal energy exchange is of natural order. However this order has been distorted with *"entitlement issues among humans"*.

As this 2nd shift occurred in 2012 to 2021 we (humans) can re-learn how to make equal energy exchange as once was brought to us.

These spirit guides continue to express that all humans, everyone on Earth has reached a new vibration from the 2nd shift that occurred in November 28, 2012. On this date the earth and moon shifted.

This was an important time for all of us humans. On August 31, 2012 there was a blue moon(a blue moon actually means 2 separate full moons in one month-it is very rare) that was profound in color. Thereafter, 2 eclipses of the moon & a star shower appeared. This was a message from Spirit guides such as Galileo about this beautiful event: *"this is a shift of human energies with the energy exchange of the cosmos."* Those same guides said, since that moment there are now *"new ways* of *asking"* for information, *"new ways to manifest"* what we (humans) would like or want in life, and **"new ways of clearing"** ourselves.

They shared that *"humans can heal on many levels using energies of the cosmos and energies of light."*
Below is one of the meditations they wanted us to utilize.

Note *Please repeat the words, if you are comfortable with them, *using the intention* (what you feel and project & desire) that "you, which is *your* true soul and *is* your pure energy and essence of "you"- that accepts and allows. I suggest you print this out and read as you visualize. You can ask your friend to read it so you can relax or local wellness center to have a group session with this detailed information. I have this mediation available on YouTube if you would like to follow my voice.

117

THE EARTH MOONS SHIFT SELF-MEDITATION:

I am (say your full name)
I allow my true soul the energy of me-to engage with my human self, body and mind-
to soul talk with my true soul energy- *all that I am energy, on all dimensions , all parallels, all that My energy exists-all energies of me in all locations.*

Take 11 deep breaths in and 11 long breaths out.

Now, if you can try to sense or feel an energetic band of golden light from the center of your stomach (solar plexus chakra-represents ego of you) Now visualize connecting that golden light that is healing energy to your heart chakra. This is located in the center of your chest. Now connect that same energetic golden light to your third eye which is the 6th chakra located in-between your eye brows on your face.

Connect another golden light connected from the 3rd eye to the top of your head; this is the 7th crown chakra. This is now connecting your mind to the energetic golden light (the all knowing you or some call it "your higher-self").

All of these points are energetically connected with a golden light like small arches from one point to the next. If you want to feel or imagine a flow of light in this golden string of vibrations, you can see it flowing back and forth. All of these connected points are *to "communicate, accept and exchange."*

This is the "human- you" connecting with the "energy of you, also known as your true soul."

I explain this to clients as the true soul of "you "it is the energy of you of when a human passes into the light , passes

118

away(deceases of life on earth) the energy of the soul continues on or elsewhere. Whether you believe your energy goes to heaven, to another dimension, or is reborn, it is the energy of the soul that goes somewhere and if you agree to that, it helps you understand the way energy can be in "places" that as humans we cannot necessarily "see" with our human eyes, but still exists as a form of energy.

 Okay back to the meditation…if you had a hard time visualizing the golden light, it is okay if you skip that part, since after reading this last paragraph I think you understand the jest of "connecting energy ."(it was connecting the human "you with the energy of your essence and communicating or placing "all of 'you' in sync"."
Please continue…by stating

"I am to be of pure energy. I, (Your full name) at this time 20_ _ (year) earth dimension bring only love into my pure energy;
 I release all blocks, all thoughts that are other than light.

I release all judgments of me and others that are other than the light.
Any and all habits that are other than the light, **I release and Exchange with positive energy**.
 At this time specifically say what you would like to "replace with positive. It can be a thought, vision or pattern. You should feel or sense the exchange and visualize or state aloud the positive outcome, make it something that replaces the negative you currently have.

 You can do one at a time, remember make it your "intention" that you truly *change and exchange it to be positive.*
 Once you have gone over and replace each and exchange the negatives to positives: read and say this directing it at "you."

"I only see myself as pure and high vibration energy which means happy, healthy and loving.
"I only allow loving relationships in my energy."

"I only allow loving energy around me."

"I am always safe and protected by loving energies."

"I allow myself and I deserve to have only positive equal energy exchange with all beings of energies, and all that is energy, including myself.
I allow and accept these "changes" in my life to be of goodness and advancement.
I only allow the light within, around and in my thoughts on this 20_ _ (year) earth dimension including *all* of where I exist, existed and reside- in all *my forms* human and beyond."

Once again take 11 deep breaths in and 11 long breaths out.
At last, give gratitude to yourself and all energies of life.

I always advise for you to drink a glass of water, take a walk place your feet flat on the floor or ground. This will bring harmony and help you feel stable after any meditation.

Interesting stuff
from Wikipedia

Matter is anything that occupies space and has rest mass (or invariant mass). It is a general term for the substance of which all physical objects consist.[1][2] Typically, matter includes atoms and other particles which have mass. Mass is said by some to be the amount of matter in an object and volume is the amount of space occupied by an object

In physics, **energy** (Ancient Greek: ἐνέργεια *energeia* "activity, operation"[1]) is an indirectly observed quantity that is often understood as the ability of a physical system to do work on other physical systems.[2][3] Since work is defined as a force acting through a distance (a length of space), energy is always equivalent to the ability to exert pulls or pushes against the basic forces of nature, along a path of a certain length.

The total energy contained in an object is identified with its mass, and energy cannot be created or destroyed. When matter (ordinary material particles) is changed into energy (such as energy of motion, or into radiation), the **mass** of the system does not change through the transformation process. However, there may be mechanistic limits as to how much of the matter in an object may be changed into other types of energy and thus into work, on other systems. Energy, like mass, is a scalar physical quantity. In the International System of Units (SI), energy is measured in joules, but in many fields other units, such as kilowatt-hours and kilocalories, are customary. All of these units translate to units of work, which is always defined in terms of forces and the distances that the forces act through.

A system can transfer energy to another system by simply transferring matter to it (since matter is equivalent to energy, in accordance with its mass). However, when energy is transferred by means other than matter-transfer, the transfer produces changes in the second system, as a result of work done on it. This work manifests itself as the effect of force(s) applied through distances within the target system. For example, a system can emit energy to another by transferring (radiating) electromagnetic energy, but this creates forces upon the particles that absorb the radiation. Similarly, a system may transfer energy to another by physically impacting it, but in that case the energy of motion in an object, called kinetic energy, results in forces acting over distances (new energy) to appear in another object that is struck. Transfer of thermal energy by heat occurs by both of these mechanisms: heat can be transferred by electromagnetic radiation, or by physical contact in which direct particle-particle impacts transfer kinetic energy.

Energy may be stored in systems without being present as matter, or as kinetic or electromagnetic energy. Stored energy is created whenever a particle has been moved through a field it interacts with (requiring a force to do so), but the energy to accomplish this is stored as a new position of the particles in the field—a configuration that must be "held" or fixed by a different type of force (otherwise, the new configuration would resolve itself by the field pushing or pulling the particle back toward its previous position). This type of energy "stored" by force-fields and particles that have been forced into a new physical configuration in the field by doing work on them by another system is referred to as potential energy. A simple example of potential energy is the work needed to lift an object in a gravity field, up to a support. Each of the basic forces of nature is associated with a different type of potential energy, and all types of potential energy (like all other types of energy) appear as system mass, whenever present. For example, a compressed spring will be slightly more massive than before it was compressed. Likewise, whenever energy is transferred between systems by any mechanism, an associated mass is transferred with it.

Any form of energy may be transformed into another form. For example, all types of potential energy are converted into kinetic energy when the objects are given freedom to move to different position (as for example, when an object falls off a support). When energy is in a form other than thermal energy, it may be transformed with good or even perfect efficiency, to any other type of energy, including electricity or production of new particles of matter. With thermal energy, however, there are often limits to the efficiency of the conversion to other forms of energy, as described by the second law of thermodynamics.

In all such energy transformation processes, the total energy remains the same, and a transfer of energy from one system to another, results in a loss to compensate for any gain. This principle, the conservation of energy, was first postulated in the early 19th century, and applies to any isolated system. According to Noether's theorem, the conservation of energy is a consequence of the fact that the laws of physics do not change over time.[4]

Although the total energy of a system does not change with time, its value may depend on the frame of reference. For example, a seated passenger in a moving airplane has zero kinetic energy relative to the airplane, but non-zero kinetic energy (and higher total energy) relative to the Earth .

TIME?

SPIRIT GUIDES SAY THERE IS "NO TIME." HUMANS INVENTED A CLOCK OR MEASURE OF TIME. THESE SPIRIT GUIDES AND ANGELS TALK OF "MOMENTS OR EXPERIENCES."

THE MEASURE OF TIME AND SPACE CAN ONLY BE KNOWN TO THOSE THAT "EXPERIENCE." OUTSIDE WHAT HUMANS KNOW AS RELATIVE SPACE, BEYOND BOUNDARIES WHAT SCIENTISTS CAN CURRENTLY CALCULATE, THERE IS WHAT THESE ANGELS AND SPIRITS CALL "MORE."

MESSAGE ABOUT THIS SHIFT IN THE EARTH AND UNIVERSE. Every 11 years a Shift cleansing "happens." This is an opportunity from the light to do a total clearing of the soul. Experiences, connections occurrence's that are to be cleansed form the soul, not just our human thoughts but the soul. No imprint of any old "junk", it is gone!

This includes habits, patterns, and occurrences and or situations. Keeping the good energy and releasing the negative energy from this life, all past and/or parallel lives depending on your beliefs. Only positive remains in the soul's energy imprint.

I was honored to be a part of this cleanse in my lifetime. You may have missed the November 2012 "window" to do this extreme cleanse. But the good news is this meditation of exchanging energy between you and others is still powerful any time you perform it. There will be another major cleanse "window "in 2023.

These spirit guides ask you not to wait for the window, do it now and you will feel the balance of your soul. By all means, do it in 2023 too!

These same guides expressed there will be another flow of information- they call it "higher knowledge." This info will be about an advanced way of healing.

Yes, more than what this book just explained. Basically the Spirits of Light messaged me "that *in 11 years many "humans will have had advanced in many ways, of healing, giving and receiving (the energy exchange, is accepted) and then 2021 there will be another advancement. this advancement has a name called 'The Humanitarian Light force '– It will be of telepathic, endearing life among humans and those who complied in the previous "time."*

They mean in 2021 this *advanced information* will be emerged at that time. Until then, the guides want us to use these healing descriptives they call *"Healing Mandalas, Light Tunnel Energy Healing, along with utilizing Reiki and Crystal energy healing." They were channeled to humans to learn how to heal themselves in these years up to that date."*

Currently, we can learn and advance. The next time will be 2021- and again in 2023.

This is not to say you can't cleanse and advance on a physical, mental, spiritual or emotional level on any day, but these specific *"windows of time"* are considered *"a clear form of cleansing the core of our energy."* -Which is deep cleansing from "carrying negative or any old junk, from this life to any other lifetime.

As I said, depending on what your belief system this 'cleanse in a certain window of time" is from this parallel (earth) to any other parallel or dimension, meaning from earth or any other realm that exists.
I was advised that learning how to soul talk to cleanse *"is a "gift of advancement from the light."*

If we as humans, "Let go, clear and cleanse", this energy it can be replaced with even, or a positive energy exchange of love, light, healthy emotions and positive thoughts.

Some of you may already know that when we have old connections that are negative, we need to release those emotions that are attached to those thoughts.

This basically means releasing the *energy* of negatives. What most people might *not* know is that we don't necessarily have to release a person from our lives. I mean you don't necessarily have to ignore them, or never talk to them again.

If you made a person feel bad *or* they made you feel bad or 'did" something negative to you or vice versa or if you both hurt each other! This person or you can have a negative attachment of energy connected to their energy field and in their souls imprint.

I will give an example:
If you have a family member that is continuously verbally abusive, you can cut the "cord or tie" of the negative emotion/energy that person "put or places" on you. You don't have to erase that person from your life to do so. You will cut those negative emotions and thoughts, from your energy field / auric bubble. You can also cut that negative emotion energy from your true souls energy imprint. Energy can be released if

you *allow it-* and you can have that person in your life and like or love them as "a family member or friend or simply as a human being".

When releasing any negative energy – it must always be *replaced* with positive. You replace the negative words, thoughts and/or actions, occurrences, situations or memories the person placed on you. If they were/are negative words or if they said them a long time ago you can always relinquish any negative emotions at any time. I would also like to add, if someone has passed on from earth. You can always change the energy between you. This is because energies exist over time and space. It can be done.

Know to **always- release, cut, and replace with positive thoughts and words; you can also use positive actions.**

Let's use a family member for an example again. When you come face to face with that family member, you already understand they are negative towards you, let their words and actions roll off you and know that it is *their* "junk" not yours- You *don't own* it!

Now that you know how to rid yourself of other peoples "junk" even if placed on you, it will not "stick". Because you only *allow love and light to stick* and that's it!

Let's say that family person was your father, so he's hard to avoid. You can always love him, for being your "father" or for being a human being, but you *don't* have to allow, accept or take on his "negative junk." Love him for being your father, not his actions or words.

Remember cutting cord & releasing is incredibly empowering, but you MUST replace unwanted or negative energy with positive energy. I say this because once you have *"owned energy"* whether it is negative or positive or null- there is "space" there, it needs to be filled with positive. If you get rid of any energy and don't replace it, that is a "void of energy." A void or empty space where energy once existed whether positive or negative, it is gone, if you allowed it and let it go. I like to describe it as there was a "space" that was currently filled; now you released or cut it out.

Energetically there is still a 'space" that exists. It is just empty or a "void of energy."

You will feel "off balance" and may go back to old ways of thinking, and "fill the voided space" with "negative replacement Junk." Previously we used the example of the family member being a negative father, it may not be the same *junk*, but you might go pick up a *significant* other that treats you the same way as the negative father did. That is filling the void NEGATIVELY. You don't want to fill it with old junk!

Okay, I hope that was understood- if you release, you replace- so make it a positive replacement! If you release a person or their actions or negative words- you can replace with something totally different. For example replace a negative person's energy with you doing something positive for you. You can do yoga, start riding a bike, cook, or try a new class that fills that time or void. These are just some healthy lifestyle examples to fill your voids, and balance your total being.

I consider a positive reconstruction of the universes energy in the earth and the atmosphere the main goal of humans to use this "energy exchange" the spirit guides brought to us in this cosmic time period. The 2nd Shift is now, since all energy is vibrations. People can change with the shifts and learn to adapt and live happy healthy lives.
These guides called Archangels, The Spirits of the light, Galileo and the Star Ones gave me a term called *"soul talking."* This is a

term they described to me is to teach people how to cleanse all the unwanted habits, thoughts, emotions from past, parallel and present.

"Talking to the souls of others. From a human/being true soul to another human/being true soul."

The soul talking- let's get back to that. This is an energy clearing- an equal or positive energy exchange of true souls. It is similar to the energy exchange with the energy of "you." This particular meditation is your true soul's energy with another's person's true soul. That is a person on earth or animal. And can also be someone whom has passed from earth.

A MEDITATION WITH YOU & OTHERS

SOUL TALKING

IF YOU HAVE, HAD OR THINK YOU HAVE NEGATIVE ENERGY BETWEEN YOU AND ANOTHER PERSON OR AN ANIMAL THIS IS FOR YOU. YEP, THAT'S YOU, IF YOU ARE HUMAN, YOU HAVE **SOMETHING TO** EXCHANGE!

SO IT'S TIME TO MAKE A POSITIVE ENERGY EXCHANGE BETWEEN YOU AND THEM TO LET GO & REPLACE WITH POSITIVE!

"Keep equal energy exchange and your life will complete as clean, cleansed and clear to advance continually. "Harmony and balance restored within self and the energy of 'self' as a true soul of light – energy. Soul talk- now."

You can do this 'soul talk" anytime it is *very* powerful, but will be incredibly powerful during a "shift window." The next shift window is year 2023.

THE SOUL TALKING- IS AN ENERGY CLEARING- A POSITIVE ENERGY EXCHANGE OF TRUE SOULS "

First step: You sit make a list. This list is of all the people things occurrences, situations, experiences that you remember as negative (hurtful to yourself, by others to you or you to them! If you find your list is quite long, that is normal. It just means you are human!)

- Note the people or animals or energy you are making the exchange do not have to be physically present. This is an energetic exchange.

Second step: Once your list is done, you relax, breathe, and take 11 deep breaths in and 11 long exhales out. Breathing in – feel the love, exhaling the negative.

Now set a positive intention and feel that you *want and allow* this exchange to happen: say aloud or in your mind:
I, _____ _____ (Your full name. First, middle, and last name. If you have a nickname or a married name add that too. Say all the names that are known as "you"!) are here to make a positive energy exchange with _____. (The person's name or visualize their face if you don't know their name.)
You can visualize that occurrence, situation, or just place an actual picture or visualize the person (or animal) or the "energy of that situation."

State the **way *you* feel**. Then state way *they* **made you feel.** With good Intention, Express fully of your emotions to release the energy of that situation. (Yes, you can cry, yell, be sorry, or all of the above and more.)

* note this process of "this cleanse" can be very intense for some

129

people. The situations or conversations can bring up anger, fear, sorrow or serenity. Please remember the spirit guides wanted me to state that *"this soul cleanse, is not about "blame, it is about releasing and replacing energy of 2 souls for an energy exchange of the light."*
If you are serious in completing this soul talking and cleanse, you will really truly "feel" the energy exchange.
That is how you know it is "working." Some people have felt it instantly during the soul talk. Many felt a sense of peace afterwards up to a few days.

Remember you can talk aloud or in the mind, this is telepathic energy which is basically the same as verbal. *" Every thought is energy."*
Then once you completed this step, continue onto

Step Three: Ask the person or animal, basically it is the "energy "of who or what you are directing this soul talking to. (Who knows, could be a tree you cut down and felt bad about it.)

Ask the energy of those souls to <u>accept this new positive</u> energy exchange of *light to replace the negative energy* that existed. Don't worry; you don't have to" hear "anything back, if you- do great. If not, keep going, it still is positive energy going out to that particular soul of that person...Please also note that if this energy is between a soul that has passed, a person whom has deceased in a human body, you can still "soul talk" to them. You can make the energy positive no matter where they are *"over space and time, energy is on all dimensions and all levels; it exists "everywhere."*

During this exchange *feel or sense* the emotions of love, solace and peace. Strongly visualize or feel the energy of forgiveness or understanding in your heart chakra (the center of your chest)- when you sense this- feel a pull in the exchanged energy to you and know they have also received the positive energy into their existence-into their energy of their soul. The guides say: *"when humans "look through others eyes, all can be resolved."*

*Note * when I personally did step 3, I visualized and drew a heart on a piece of paper and pretended I handed it to that person across from me and visualized in my mind that they accepted it and I then felt this amazing sensation over my heart and chest area, it then traveled through my entire body it was amazing.*

Step Four: Close out the conversation of energy by thanking them and give gratitude for this opportunity with them to make amends and state that *"both of your true souls have made an even and Positive energy exchange to be equal".* Say your goodbyes and Breathe in and out fully for 11 breaths.

Step Five: Congratulations are in order, Know that you are successful in the exchange. Know that you deserve this positive energy as they do too.
Take a break and do a few more on your list, if any.

You are on your way to *"advancement of a true soul."*
You will notice in the next few days a *"change"* in your energy, the guides say: *"humans will feel lighter- peaceful."*

Note * I have received many emails from people all over the world doing the soul talking & energy exchanges. They shared amazing results some were very extremes cases. One woman hadn't heard from her father in years, and a week after the meditation he called her on the phone, out of the blue, having a nice conversation that was not of the norm from him. The woman was happy just to hear from him.
Another received a message / omen from an animal guide that let her know her son was in the light. So many people have

shared their positive exchanges and felt they too have shifted into a better place in their lives. I am glad they shared the information, gratitude.

ENTITLEMENT OR ENERGY EXCHANGE?

If someone gives you something, whether it is a book to borrow or a smile do you automatically think" what does that person want from me?"
Have you ever "expected" another person to give you something, if you give them something? I am not talking about a purchase at a store that is a different story. I am talking about "the thought or thinking" that if you want something, which you will intentionally "think" that you deserve something in return, other than the words of "thank you".
The world is a funny place, well at least on earth. I notice every day in conversations with other people that most do assume that if you do something or offer a favor, the other person feels indebted to give you something psychically back of the same value.

Is that an energy exchange? Yes, it is. But is it a positive energy exchange when we "expect someone to give us something only because you are giving to them? No. That is not a positive *intention* with the energy exchange.
A positive energy exchange is when I offer you something, let's say a tangible object, and let's say cookies. I bought chocolate cookies and I am offering you one to eat or take, I do this without thinking you owe me, or thinking next time *you* have food or something that you owe me.

The gesture was innocent, but TV and our society reaks that we have to *give to get. Society trains us and makes us think that* "I will only do something to help you if you do something for me."

This is a selfish way of existence.

A positive energy exchange is a smile; I smile at you, you at me.
I want to offer you a cookie, you say "thank" and I smile.
No agenda, no debt.
There's a reason we gave that word, "debt" a bad cognation...
"Debt "it means "owes" the words inventively sounds negative
or bad.

The good or positive energy exchange has the intention that is
thoughtless or simply kind, or lighthearted, not expectant or
preplanned in the way of wanting return value. It is hard today
because it is automatic with most of us. It happened to me and I
fell into it.

I found myself years ago when I owned a wedding flower
business. I only got referrals from larger companies, such as
hotels and party planners if I gave them a kick back (money). I
was rated #1 in my area for my expertise, but they still only sent
me business if I slipped them money without "other" people at
their establishment knowing. After 18 years in that business, I
was disgusted at myself for paying some of them and disgusted
because I was part of that negative exchange that made me feel
yucky and used. The point that only with the exchange of monies
to be able to "work" at those venues, made me feel like all my
heard work was irrelevant in complimenting my hard work.(I
am thankful however all my brides were thankful and their
happiness on the day of their marriage made up for the other
negative exchanges. During my "flower days" my best way of
gaining business was word of mouth by my brides I provided
with the best service and products. I love flowers and that
industry, but that one part of it, I could do without.

Although I was successful, I felt the energy exchange between those particular people discerning. I decided I wasn't going to "play that game." I found I felt so much happier in my work. Today in my business owner of a Mindful healing center, very few people come to "play that negative exchange," most come with whole hearts and simply exchange as it was way in the past, as trade, or true kindness without entitlement. Take time to notice yourself and people around you, try to make the energy between you and others positive and stop that mindless process of thinking, make kind gesture and let go of "expecting." Life is much easier this way.

10 Things You Should Know When Exploring Your Psychic Intuition

Have you been thinking a lot lately or have you received some "signs" to start exploring your intuitive senses? Most of us come to a point where we ask or want to ask someone—anyone—how does it work? What exactly is intuition? Do I have it? Does everyone have it? Can I control it? There are so many questions regarding this beautiful mysterious part of your life (and the beyond).

My mission is to make sure everyone can have the tools they need to help them in preparation for the 2nd Big Shift and to keep them feeling safe. Let's face it, the unknown can be scary. I've had several occasions where I thought I might be crazy or thought I was talking to myself inside my head. Sometimes I felt as if I was taking on emotions of everyone around me, which I later found out was my ability for psychic empathy. Understanding basic information about your psychic intuition through guidance of exploring yourself is very important.

I wrote this chapter because when I first started exploring my intuition, I had so many questions. I attended many spiritual classes and read countless books to discover this specific information. Hopefully, I am saving you a lot of time and money by writing what I've learned.

If I could have had this bit of information lumped all into one source, I would've been further ahead on my spiritual journey. I would have advanced much sooner in learning and understanding about the spiritual world. Now I am sharing **10 main things you should know when exploring your psychic Intuition**. I hope this is helpful to you.

10 THINGS YOU SHOULD KNOW
<u>KNOWLEDGE IS KING</u>

1 INTENTION

This is the *most important* to me and should be to all of us. Intention is the thought, the visualization to really mean what you are saying, thinking, feeling or doing with all your heart and soul.

Simply put**, Intention is what you desire and project** during your work, prayers, light work, healing or intuitive readings, and just every day in your life. While doing whatever it is you are doing or thinking, add "intention"; care about what you are doing, emotionally; "feel" what you are doing or thinking. That is what I call Intention.

Why is intention important aside from helping to make you a better person? Because it's important to have good intentions when connecting to your source so that your outcomes are positive. Intention is the key to reaching your intuition and spiritual explorations

I hope you are only giving love, light or both to your intentions—keeping the "light" in your work or thoughts.

I apply Intentions to all I do, and ask anyone if they can tell the difference in my work when I don't. It is amazing how Intention—this positive emotional high vibrational energy—can change your life and others for the better.

Energy, we are all energy—all made of vibrations which are energy. Think of music, the vibrations you hear are energy waves that we can't see, but feel and hear. We all have different energies. Some of us are soft, light, and comfy. Some of us are louder, bolder, stronger. It doesn't matter. If the intentions of whatever you are doing or placing the intention on are good, no matter what your energy is, it is high vibration. When an intention is good, good is from the light and light is high vibration. So, good intentions are high vibrations. If you are an energy sucker—a vampire as some say—your intentions may not be in the light, and probably not on purpose. However, once you are mindful you realize that everyone can connect to their source. When I say "source" I'm talking about positive energy, mother earth, and/or your god. You can channel this energy from the light source without taking from others. Reiki is a modality of this teaching or energy healing. There are several modalities you may research and learn.

Let's talk about sensing energies.

Do you know how you can walk up to someone and instantly know that they are in a bad mood or spewing negative? Immediately your body tends to move away from this person because you feel their energy field, which is a low vibration. It doesn't mean they will always be of low vibration; it is just you sensing that person's negative emotions in their energy field at that particular time. When a person is truly happy they are of higher vibrations and, of course, when they are unhappy the energy surrounding them can be of lower vibration.
You want high vibration energy, which begins with good loving Intention.

2 ASKING

Asking is one of the most effective ways of manifesting your loving thoughts or affirmations. It sounds too easy, and yes, it actually is easy!

When you ask the universe and state precisely what you are asking for (as long as it is in loving ways with good Intention) you are placing that good energy out to the universes and spirit world, and yes, also yourself. This becomes an affirmation or prayer. This is positive programming for you and the universes to hear the vibrations so that the ask or request can be heard and acknowledged.

When asking, make sure your Intention is for the greater good of all involved, be truthful and honest about what you are asking, and don't forget to visualize the outcome as it has already come true. I always finish my asking of the universe with a "thank you" and blessing. But a "thank you" will suffice, being grateful for the actions to be manifested helps tremendously.

For example:
If you are currently in poor health, you may ask, "Universe, I am asking to be healthy on all levels, physically, mentally emotionally and spiritually." "I am asking specifically for my knee, specifically for my left knee to be in perfect working order for full range of motion of my left knee." You will be asking with loving intention and visualize yourself well. You can picture yourself running on the beach, your knee is well and you, as a whole, are feeling well and your body is working perfectly!

Ok I know this ask sounds wordy, but, the more detailed information or specific information you state and the more you visualize the outcome, the better the message can be understood.

Think of it this way, if you were hearing a rumor, it probably has passed through several people before you heard it. Do you think it was as accurate as when it first started? Probably not. As the rumor passes through many storytellers, the story changes a bit here and there. It's kind of like a fishing story. Somehow as the story goes on, the fish becomes bigger and bigger depending who is telling the story or the catch becomes more difficult. I think you get what I'm going for here. There's another very important message here: Make sure your Intentions are true! Use only positive wording or you will get what you ask for without knowing you asked for it!

Here's an example of what **NOT** to do. This ask is using negative connotation:
"Dear universe can I have a rich man to meet, but **not** with bad health or small house , I want him to be good and **not** mean."

This is an incorrect way of asking. You are using negative connotation by using "**not**". Spirit guides and others in the spirit world do not hear negative connotations well, so they hear that you want a rich man with bad health or small house. State what you want from a positive point of view.

Using positive loving intentions and your mind can be very powerful thing.

When asking the universe you should state your ask with positivity in both directions. In other words, ask for your future husband to be respectful to you and that you'll be respectful to him; this creates a balance of energies, this creates a "positive energy exchange." Here is that same scenario asked correctly:

"Please, I ask the universe for this with loving intentions. I am and I allow myself to meet and marry an attractive man who is abundant in money, is in good health, has healthy habits, owns a nice home, is caring, respectful and has a wonderful sense of humor. I am and I allow myself to be respectful to him, I also am attracted to him and we have similar sense of humor and we are happy together in a loving relationship. Thank you. I am grateful."

Remember to be confident in asking and make sure you keep feeling that the intention is true. I often hear clients say, "I said the positive affirmation" and I always follow up with asking them, "Did you mean it? When you said your affirmation, did you feel it?" I also ask them: Did you think that you deserve what you asked for? As you asked and after you finished asking?" Most of the time a client will say, "No, I didn't feel like I truly deserved what I was asking for." I can't tell you how much it means for you to place the true intention and feeling it- You have to believe in what you're asking for. Be confident. Everyone deserves good things!

There *is also another part* of asking you need to understand, other than affirmations, there is the mystery voice or noise.

Let's say, for example, that you sort of "hear" things and you are not sure if they are coming from you, in your head, or they are from an outside source. The first thing you should do is ask, "Are you from the light"? Immediately the "voice "should say "yes." If "no" or you hear nothing then please refer to the Protection section below immediately! If "yes," then that is great.

If you are at the point of your intuitive exploration where you can hear, then it's very important to ask the "voice" who they are and what their intentions are. Are they from the light, spirit guides, angels?

Now ask, "What is your name?" If they don't give you a name, be patient, maybe they want you to name them so you can identify with them by what makes you comfortable. Ask if they are here for a specific purpose, to help you maybe become a healer, to teach you, or to help you with some lesson you might have to learn.

At this this point, your receiving a name is not important as you know you have spiritual contact with either your higher self, or an angel, spirit, spirit guide or loved one from the light. So be thrilled and happy!

Now, I have come across several people who have outside sources they discovered that are not their higher-self speaking to them and, by the way, have been yelling at them! The most likely reason these people are being yelled at by these spirits is that the spirits are feeling ignored. Once you have asked and confirmed that a spirit is from the light, and then you can ask them to please stop yelling because you can hear them now and are going to listen to what guidance they have for you. If you are a person that just hears "noise" it may be several spirits talking at once, maybe hundreds! This means you have to ask them to only speak one at a time, after all, you are only human!

I had one client whose guide was yelling so loud she had gotten headaches. I reviewed the whole process of "asking" with my client and told her to ask her guide if her guide was female because my client told me she had a female voice. I suggested that she ask the guide nicely (always be courteous and nice, you wouldn't speak to anyone if they were rude) to please, if she could create an accent, like an English accent, so she could distinguish her guide from her own thoughts. It worked! Her guide was so nice and accommodating she started expressing with an English accent to help my client. They now have a great relationship!

All in all, don't be afraid to ask and communicate truthfully with your guides or visitors from the light. They are guides; they want to give you "guidance". They are here to show you positive options only and because you are of free will you can always make your own decision—always. If you don't "hear" per say a spirit or guide, you may "feel" their presence. This feeling can be warm, or an indication of positive vibrations, in your presence. If you find that the spirit who you view as a guide is telling you what to do with your life in a demanding or negative way, or if you get a bad energy feeling around you, please go directly to the "7. Protection" section later in this chapter and read it, and re-read it! Remember, if this spirit or the energy of

140

that spirit, contacting you feels negative then protect yourself and don't communicate with them.

Now you are communicating with the Light energies, this is great!

Here's an exercise you can use to practice, and can be done alone or with a group.

Asking the Universe

This is a session where a group works together with visualizations, by "Asking the Universe" for what we need or want for ourselves or another. You can do this exercise with just yourself or a group, both are very powerful.

First, we say the following words together and afterwards, each person will take a turn to state a request to the universe as if it has already been manifested. After which, all as a group (or you can) "imagine or picture" that request for the person who asked the universe. Approximately one minute each.

In the steps below, state #1 through #4 together as a group, then each person will make their request at step 5. Once everyone has made their requests and visualized the request, the group will say #6 and #7 together with loving intentions. You can do this alone if you don't have a group. Of course group visualization would be more powerful, but even alone it is extremely powerful.

Say Together:

1. We come here today to ask the universe for guidance.
2. We ask with only loving intentions to manifest our requests.
3. We are powerful, loving and strong. We wish only the best for all those involved in our requests and for the greater good of all involved.
4. We are always safe and surrounded by Love.

5. **Each person, individually, makes their request.**

   After each person's request we say together:

6. The Universe has heard your request_____ (person's name) and is fulfilling your needs for the greater good of all involved.

   After we all have asked the universe for our request we say together:

7. We are grateful. Thank you, Universe, for the loving energy you send our way. We have projected powerful loving affirmations as a group by visualizing in Loving Light and manifested these requests to be true and realized. Positive energy surrounds us and the universe. We understand the universe will hear our requests and fulfill them as they are powerful, positive and loving.

8. **Manifesting for you: "life" as you want it is best.** Be detailed in what you want and positive vibration in how you think or say these with intentions(true feelings) that you want, and deserve these things or people in your life with an equal" energy exchange"

   Example: There is detailed information on manifesting on pages 95-96.

9. *I am and allow myself (this wording avoids self-sabotage)* to marry a man that has healthy habits, he is (physically, sexually and mentally) attracted to me and I to him, he is intelligent, humorous, is abundant in money, he loves me as much as I love him, we are monogamous to each other, he believes in me and I in him, we are compatible and happy together. We trust each other, we are monogamous and only to each other. I deserve this in my life now, this year 20__ _"(example: 2014 earth dimension)

10. You can add or delete what you wish but only use high vibration words, and remember even a thought is energy and can manifest or negate what you desire. So after you say this affirmation, Please know and think and say that you deserve it and you deserve each other, otherwise a simple thought such as you in your head saying" well, if it happens," THAT just negated it! This energy went out to the universe as null or nugatory. "Believe it and know it-"everyone deserves good things in life, including you!

3 Accepting

Allow yourself to believe there is more out there beyond human life forms. This is important.

Accepting the information you receive from your guide without freaking yourself out is a big plus. You must learn to allow yourself to accept help from others; it doesn't make you weak, it makes you stronger. This is not as easy as it sounds. Learning to accept the information you receive requires trust.

I like to give the following example because there are a lot of people out there that are "givers", as I like to say. When you are always giving that is nice; it makes you feel great! So why do "givers" have such a hard time accepting? We all know a friend, or maybe this is you, who refuse a gift or favor by saying, "No, no I'm good, please take it back." By not accepting the gift or gesture that person who didn't accept or say thank you just took the feeling of "goodness" from the giver. I'm sure you know what giving feels like; it feels really good, but by not accepting the gesture you just denied that person the positive emotion. That's not nice! What the givers have to realize is that it makes others feel good to give. So, accept! Givers also have to realize the difference between accepting and taking. There is a huge difference! If you are being offered, it is not taking! Please, all you givers learn to accept as well. It makes others feel good.

This was also explained by the guides in the "energy exchange" messages.

4 Trusting

Trusting is about yourself and your true feelings—your intuitiveness. Just trust. Leave your doubts and insecurities at the door and see how much stronger you are, but remember to only be stronger in loving ways with good loving intentions for all involved, including the universes.

Trusting your source and *yourself* will help you understand this whole "communication" or contact from the other dimensions thing. Even if you decide all this information is not for you, that's cool. Please still learn to trust yourself. That little voice or feeling you have to go right instead of left, just try it, listen and do, see if it brings you goodness. Trusting yourself is one of the most beautiful things you can do for yourself. It brings confidence in all you do. Practice trusting you.

5 Sacred Space

A sacred space or place is important because it makes you feel safe and helps you tap into your psychic intuition comfortably. I believe that if we all had our own little sacred place, we would all be much less stressed in today's world. Find a place in your home, outside, or even at a beach or park. Go to this place at least a few times a week or when you feel you really need some "me" time. Use this location to meditate and release any feelings that are not positive. You also can use this place to ask the universe, renew your energy, and recite your affirmations and gratitude to others and your loving beliefs.

Having a sacred space is amazing. It can be in your home or your yard, it could be the beach or anywhere that you feel safe, comfortable and can relax. Once you found this space, big or small (my friend's sacred space is in the closet so the kids can't find her), make this space yours by adding some little things like a few gemstones or a picture of a vacation place that made you feel "Zen". This is a space that you know you can go to and just breathe. If you decide to start contacting your guides or asking the universe for anything you can be sure this is a good place where you can place good intentions to do so.

Some people like to make their "space" like an altar, placing flowers for themselves and their guides, lighting candles, misting some essential oils, burning incense. It's all good as long as you feel good there. This is your "happy place". If you have a good imagination or visualization skills you can always bring your sacred place with you by using your mind to visualize and bring it to wherever you go. I actually do this a lot.

6. Clearing

Everyone has heard of clearing space, right? Not cleaning, but clearing. But it is kind of similar. Clearing your space means energetically cleaning auric debris from the electromagnetic field or the aura and other energies that surround your body. The space can be the space surrounding your body, your home, work or whatever space you occupy. Clearing helps you stay balanced physically, mentally, emotionally, spiritually, and help you receive messages clearer.

You can clear by sage-ing or using your good/loving intentions to keep your home or yourself (body, mind, emotions and your auric field) cleansed so that you and your surroundings remain on higher vibrations.

*note you can clear space and your body with actual sage, rose oil or rose water. A mixture of herbs or essences is a great way to cleanse too. These can be applied to the body, inhaled or spritzed! These are just add-ons, you have to use intention of thought when using that "they are clearing me and my space."

We are all made up of energy, everything is made of energy. Energy is vibrations. Vibrations of high frequency are not

that. I totally turn it around and I see the *good* of what might have happened for me or for the good of another.

Remember everything is not all about you. Leaving our egos behind is quite hard, but when you do, you will feel and see the difference it makes in your life.

You can let go of things like jealousy. It truly is amazing. You become happier with "you", you feel more content with what you have and have to offer yourself physically and mentally. It's like this beautiful gift inside us, that we just need to release, or open that window so we can see it clearly.

You need to show your higher vibrations and happiness to yourself and the world around you, and of course beyond. The more you open your mind and beliefs, the more you can explore and decide what is right for you.

You may not believe all you hear from gurus and psychics, but that may be because that information was meant for them and others, but not you. You are meant to experience, feel, or hear what is right for you and your life. This comes from the soul of "you." The expression "different strokes for different folks" applies here!

Basically, you must believe in yourself and be able to identify what is positive and trust yourself to believe in that. Believe in positive vibrations and positive information.

10 Explore

Continue to explore. Exploration is the key to finding what modalities are right for you. Maybe you want to learn Reiki for self-healing, maybe you just want to know about it or possibly you want or feel the need to help others with it as a profession. You may also be feeling you need to know more so you can teach and spread what you have learned and add to what you had already felt.

Begin to open up to hear what others say or experience. Make life more fun and exciting, open up to conversations with others you find have positive energy so you can find enjoyment of others and then share your experiences that may help each other. Experiences make us well-rounded. Take a chance and live outside your box.

Here are some things to know and services you can explore.

AFFIRMATIONS & INTENTIONS

Affirmations are prayers or positive statements to achieve higher vibration. Intention is what you desire and project of a verbalization or thought.

CHAKRAS

Chakras are energy centers that are located down the center of a person's body along the meridian or spinal column. These wheel or discs like centers are also associated with colors for each chakra point. There are 7 main chakras but there are over 144,000 chakras in the human body. . These are energy centers that constantly open and close on a day to day basis.

**A Bit More on Chakras & our
energy exchange with our human Bodies**

The 7 main energy centers called chakra points

Each Chakra represents a center point in the human body which can energize, release, hold or vibrate. Of which, these centers constantly open and close during the day which is normal, but keeping them balanced is the key to being a balanced human. When I say balanced, I mean psychically, mentally emotionally and spiritually balanced.

When humans are unbalanced in anyone of these areas for a

long period of time, sickness can manifest- it could be as physical, mental, emotional or spiritual. So keeping your "self" aligned and balanced is a must. The chakra at the base of the spine is called the root or 1st chakra, representing 'grounding". The 2nd chakra, Sacral representing "survival, instinct", The 3rd chakra is solar plexus representing "personal Power or EGO", The 4th chakra , the heart, representing Love and compassion, the 5th chakra the throat chakras representing communication, expression , creativeness and also listening" The 6th chakra representing the "third eye" or mind's eye this represents intuitiveness and trusting in yourself.

Lastly, the 7th chakra which represents connection to your higher self the all knowing you, and the celestial plane of Angels, Spirit guides, and humans that have passed over or on other dimensions.

Knowing more about your body is excellent way of certain balance or energy exchange with yourself on level that is physical and mental along with spiritually. Taking good care of your physical body is part of the exchange as well. You most likely feel healthier or "better" when you eat foods that are known as natural or organic, basically unprocessed. That is a positive energy exchange with your insides and outside on the physical level. Your chakras are the example of the perfect energy exchange on an energetic level.

INTENTION
Intention is what you desire and project. Intention is the key to psychic channeling, readings, guidance and information. This is the most important piece of knowledge in life, intention and knowing how to use it for goodness.

MEDITATION
Meditation is all about relaxing your mind and body, and letting

all that is in your thought of reality go. Empty your mind so you can just "be" or to help you to receive messages from any Light entities or your higher-self. It is basically when you forget about what time it is.

MEDITATION CIRCLES
Most of the time at spiritual or growth/wellness centers usually have classes or call them "circles" where you can meditate with a group. There are 3 or more persons in a group like this, sometimes they are guided meditations other times they just use crystals, gemstones or sounds like crystal singing bowls, drums or gongs.

HEALING CIRCLES
Healing circles are groups that meet to give and receive healings usually using the modalities of Reiki, Light Tunnel energies, or Light Touch techniques. These are techniques that are learned from a higher trained person or certified instructor.

A FEW CHANNELED "MESSAGES"
Messages from Arch Angel Michael, The Spirits of the Light, The Light Ones, St. Germain and spirit master called EROM

"Energy cannot be duplicated. That is why a soul is only original. You cannot copy a soul. The same with the energy of a soul. An example would be an energy healer- they channel energies of the light-through their soul and human casing (body). This brings the energy uniqueness that no other can duplicate.

This is the reason humans are attracted to other humans in several ways- not only human traits such as personality and looks but soul traits that are unique energies of which each soul has "energy of the soul is what another soul senses, feels as human or non-human and is attracted to the high vibrations of the soul core that cannot be duplicated.

153

Humans found a way to duplicate vibrations of sounds- but not soul energies. It will never be done. Cloning is not cloning of a soul, only its structure (body)."

Another important message

Energies such as entities have auras like we have auras, these also called as the electromagnetic field which surrounds our bodies on earth. If a spirit is on this dimension there aura or electromagnetic field can be felt by some sensitive humans also may be called psychics, empaths mediums or intuitives. I can give an example many people I channel messages for ask me and the guides "I have been feeling a presence that feels dark or don't know... not good. "So we ask them so you are identifying that the energy that surrounds you is negative to you.

They say yes. Basically what is happening whatever spirit or entity is present is in their auric field and is letting them know they the entity doesn't want you in that space for whatever reason, and there can be many) such as for example the entity may have been human and passed away suddenly and didn't realize they were no longer in human form, but care still on the earth dimension- no one can see them, and they see you in their home or space. I would be angry too.

What I'm getting at is that this entity is mad. This can make your aura feel uneasy or sense that same emotion "mad." If they are in your auric field feeling mad and you can feel or sense this emotion because your aura and this deceased (spirits energy) persons aura is in touch with yours. That is how you sense it, the presence of this ghost, deceased person. It is also true when you sense a loving spirit, deceased or angel; you feel a good emotion or sensations, and some even see "light, or figures of light.

Those who are very sensitive and visual can actually see an angel or entity and deciphering if it is good or bad feeling on an energetic level. All and all this is how we can sense these

154

energies through our auric energies our auric fields. They are like our fingerprints they can identify ourselves and others. I also explain them to be patterns of energy which are basically are vibrations that we feel as emotions.

I have a client that comes often to receive energy healings. Every week she comes and says she's is always confused and feels bad. Sometimes it's emotional, sometimes psychical. She currently sees an herbalist, and counselor and acupuncturist and me for energy healing and channeling. It's been about 3 months she's been coming I have seen progress but I was watching her interactions with others and at first I thought she just needed attention, whether it was from her talking of her unknown illnesses or for getting involved with other people's lives perhaps because she was lonely at this time in her life.

Yesterday in a channeling session with the angel archangel Michael, he said to her" you are and empathic.
now we already established this when she first started coming but, this is what he said to her next" you constantly pick up co-workers, friend, neighbors, just anyone you talk to or pass, you pick up their energies." I knew exactly what he was saying. He went on to say you never let go of these, psychical or emotionally." You don't know how *you* feel because you only are feeling others pains and emotions whether happy or =sad or aches etc., you are confused anyone would be, you cannot feel YOU."

My client's eyes lit up as mine did, it totally made sense. All these doctors she was seeing even the herbalist said I can't find anything I don't know why you feel like you do, of course because every day she thought she had some different alignment, a knee pain ,and stomach ache then emotional trauma.

It was a light that went off, we realized all these were the people she surrounded y and not only that, she would pick up emotions

155

from reading a book that had expresses dangers and abnormal behaviors which she took on as her own!

I am also and empath, I was self-taught to first identify where the emotion or pain is coming from, once I establish that is not mine , I immediately let go of this emotion or psychical pain. (I keep the happy feelings lol) I told my client how she can "release anything that is other than the light," meaning anything that is not good from anyone or any entity book, TV you name it. I taught her to know "if it's not yours- don't own it!" She learned how to trust herself in doing so.

I gave her this scenario, if she <u>didn't</u> bump her toe and her toe does hurt, it most likely is **not** her pain to bear. There was no self-*cause* of the pain. She empathically picked up that the cause of her painful toe was from someone who was having pain in their toe. She was sensing this energetically from the other persons toe pain.

She was simply absorbing the negative emotion and physical pain from the other persons auric energy. She realized she was standing next to person that had a "toe injury" at that time. She learned *to identify and realize, then allowed herself let go of a negative* that was not hers to own, energetically speaking. Today she is fine and feels great, no need for countless doctors. She is maintaining her health and is very happy instead of confused. She knows how and what she feels today and every day. What a relief for her! Thank you Archangel Michael!

This is a Channeled message from 10/30/11 about the years 2012 and beyond.

The dimensions are getting thicker, due to the energy exchange in the atmosphere, the planets are moving and other dimensions are feeling this as we are on earth. The change or part of the New 2nd shift is nearing. As we spoke there are many changes to affect the earth within the tectonic plates and also with the air changing.

To understand the changes of the dimensions is all of energy and the positive energies that are put out and surrounding these dimensions. The change overall is letting sensitive people on earth feel this and know the changes are coming soon, our human bodies can sense it and want to adapt. Early human's learned to adapt to weather conditions (and more), we know will have the same evolution of adapting to the new air, the new way of life. The atmosphere is changing from planets and planetary destruction, meaning that many planets are affected by ours earth. Earth has been as I say self-destruct due to human inadequacies, but also because its structure has been compromised.

With this humans "moved" too many sections or parts of this earth and for this along with the planetary pulls will start as it already has in the first shift and will continue to self-destruct piece by piece from above the earth and below the earth until it has been renewed".

Everything affects everything on all dimensions. We are all energies that occupy the universes and beyond. Each should be responsible for what is happening, but overall our planet the worst meaning used in an inadequate way will try to be saved. Other entities come to teach us how to adapt to this new earth we will encounter in this future. Occurrence by occurrence we will change, we will have to, teach the young to learn skills that can communicate with other life beings on other dimensions and these same beings are teaching many of us all over the worlds we know as earth to communicate and, adapt and teach us movement of energy so we can "move" to another atmosphere if we prove we will not self-destruct it as earth has been.

When they mean "move" they are saying that our physical bodies can adapt but our souls, our minds and energies our auric field containing our souls can move into other dimensions to "live" in new worlds if needed by the self-destruction of the earth.

In short, we need to be happy, live happily and be good to the earth and each other. This will make positive changes in all worlds that exist.

"Let your high vibrational energy emit to be of the Light"

I was advised by the Guides of Light, to share a channeled message from 11-11-11 that they had previously given to me on that date. They said *"to share it again, the message of 11-11-11 in this book.* They said *"this was a strong message that needs to be heard and realized over and over and over again!"* I believe that's why they gave it on the date 11-11-11.

The channeled message said:

"As the shift continues of the need for humans to work together to keep vibrations high, also meaning happiness, in their emotions other than negative emotions which bring low vibrational energies that will surround the atmosphere and result in movement of the planetary world."

This is a healing-it will progress. The planetary shift is here-you will feel more changes- we know you have felt many changes already in the last couple years- as you have written, it will be the truth- prepare-spread the word of the new world to come adaptation to new air-of dimensional changes all of us alike will adapt. To listen to our guidance as it will be of the light and is needed greatly for healing to come all humans, all-life, planets, atmospheres together life force exists and will continue in other forms.

We see that each human has individual needs. You will find that "healing work" you do will increase of the number of humans meaning they will increase in needing alternative light energies to adapt, survive and carry existence, survival is known to

158

humankind. It will always exist. We share guidance to redeem the light as many misconstrue the messages as dark- we are only here in light and love to create, preserve and inherently show force of energy surround earth and humans as vibrational pull of the atmosphere is and will change as told to you in 2021. It has started. Be well we will guide you as needed. Amen-"

Sequential Numbers 1 or 11

Since the numbers 11-11 always seem to be "noticed" for me and millions of others around the globe, I would like to share that sequential numbers are quite common in many of us. Seeing sequential numbers can give us great insight on what is going on in our life.

I have been working with numbers and the Spirit guides have confirmed that the number 11 means "making a decision, good from bad, right from wrong. " If you see doubles of the number 11 it is intensified. This meaning, "I really need to make that decision sooner!" Because it has been noticed repeatedly-you are taking longer than it should to make that important decision.

If you see a number 1 , that means "letting go, let life flow, also taking charge of one's life to bring more loving energy into it." The spirits stated "you have to recharge yourself with positive energy after you let go."

Ponder this....

Energy exchange with Angels & spirits

It's important if you want to "communicate with Angels or spirits that you have good intentions. It is especially important that you *do not have* "distorted" energy. My description of "distorted energy" is someone who is abusing their body, mainly the function of the human brain. Yes, this means a glass of wine, a toke, trippin or anything remotely close. All of these "things" distort energy. It distorts your energy in a way that brings insecurities, fear and can also make telepathic communication or "visual messages from the "mind's eye" *inaccurate* to say the least!

Some people that can sense or see auras of humans can feel or see the electromagnetic field that surrounds our human bodies. These readers of auras can "see" or sense a grey, icky yuck around a person who has 'distorted' their energy field.

With this said, when conversing, telepathically to a spirit guide or Angel your information will most likely be 'heard wrong." Many times an angel wont visit, they will stay away rather than having you interpret the information and guidance in a misconstrued manner.

If you are a person who uses 'tools' such as pendulums, oracle card decks for guidance or readings, my suggestion is make sure you are not under the 'influence." This distorted energy is considered dirty because most people whom use drugs or alcohol can be holding a lower vibration due to insecurities of themselves or of life in those moments of usage. This can be why if you are trying to use an oracle deck or pendulum to do a self-reading and you don't believe or trust the answer or message you received. You may find yourself saying: "My message wasn't clear and I didn't feel like it is accurate!"

This is not to down on having some fun, but to me would you ask a doctor to perform a surgery on you if he's drunk? You have to feel what is true to yourself; trust is a main part of receiving information from spirits and angels. This is also my reasoning about going to a healing center for an energy healing session; would you want a healer to have distorted energy flowing in your energy field?

This is a "no. no." with the Angels and spirit guides. *"Stay of pure energy to receive the pure accurate messages of the light."* A message straight from the Angels themselves. They wanted this quote in this book.

To make an equal energy exchange with Angels or spirits guides, it's quite simply put in this message: *We will help you, if you ask us accurately and with loving intentions for all involved, without ego and pure, clean energy.*
That is how they would like to "exchange" with us as humans.

Universes and parallels
 this concept of the energy exchange can be a bit confusing since the information given about parallels and universes existing other than earth can be hard to grasp.
 The exchanges between them as I was told (yes again by angel and spirits) that all of us exist with **"different time and space" energy is still the same, it is powerful and great, but to exchange purity is best to be accepted as even or positive."**

I have learned from my career with energy healing and reading as a conduit, that many of us have instances or situations that we "feel" that we have had, but not always sure it was from this life. As we grow and live, we 'sense "these occurrences or situations to be a "lesson."

Lessons move us out of one part of our life or our life's view- and *into new* ways of "seeing or experiencing" life. I strongly feel this is happening as our energy of our existence can be in more than one place at a time. Our dreams and thoughts along with déjà vu can make most of us think deeper about our lives. About how, why and where we can be and what we learn on a human earthly day to day basis.

 The notion of past lives or parallels is intriguing since it is hard to prove, but easy to believe.
 Each of us decides for ourselves until those "coincidences happen" and can *change* our minds or help us realize that "energy" can travel. Kind of like the cell phones energy waves, we cannot see them but they travel and exist. Because we have flesh and bones our bodies make us grounded to earth, but our,

161

minds, thoughts and true soul of energy can travel to distance places. After all they are just vibrations.

For me and many other people, these "travels" seem very real in meditations, sleeping or hypnosis. How can so many people make this stuff up?

Especially when visions have so much detail, how can it be proven?

Details come through about a lot of places on earth that currently exists but when locations where I have never been appear along with seeing people's faces I never knew, that's amazing.

Some visions or travels of the minds energy is proof to me that we can connect with unknown "places" that don't seem to be of this planet earth but beyond.
The energy exchange with other realms, dimension, parallels or past lives to me are relevant that energy is "energy." In all those that exist-are in my mind or "experiences of energy vibrations".

To exchange thought or dreams with what energy exists within them is amazing to evaluate. In my experiences and also discussed with many of my clients there are "lessons or learning" within our minds travels and the "experience of these places" is proof enough that a positive exchange is pertinent there too.

One revelation on parallels is that our human body can be on earth dimension, but our energy body and mind can be on another at the same moment parallel dimension.

Is this what absent minded "is?"

One of my example's: Have you ever misplaced an item? Let say your glasses. You know you placed them on the table by the door, but now they aren't there in that spot. You may have asked others "have you seen my glasses, I know I put them there on that table?" They reply, "No haven't seen em." Then five hours

162

later they are in that spot you originally thought you placed them.

No, really you aren't as disorganized as you thought- or were you temporarily in a parallel? People used the old expression "are *absent minded*?" I like that expression; most old sayings are somewhat true. My notion: You *were* in the *same place* but a parallel of that same place in between a moment. I know it sounds tricky, but it's truly plausible.

Maybe that's where the old expression "precious moments" came from????

Remember, if you
"Look through others eyes, the world will be exchanged as proper liking to all."

BONUS

Do ya want to learn how to manifest with equal energy in detail? Do read on…

MANIFESTING EQUAL ENERGY EXCHANGE

How would you like to receive all that you desire?
I am sure you have heard of "Affirmations." That is when you verbally repeat something you want in your life. Another way is to pray for what you want. That is, of course, if you believe in other sources that are mightier than humans.
I realized if I want to receive what I want or desire, whether I ask the Universe, pray to Angels or higher sources, that it is possible. I believe all of us can ask and manifest what we want. However, I was clairaudiently taught by these higher beings that "asking" must be done with equal energy exchange."

What is Equal energy? What do I mean that I was told?

163

First of all, a person that can sense vibrational messages through hearing is a clairaudient. You probably heard of a clairvoyant. That's more common. A clairvoyant can see, hear, feel, and smell, basically using all their senses to receive messages or information.

It also is identifying vibrations which is energy on a different level than most humans can relate to. This information comes from sources other than human or from another realm, dimension, parallel or all of the above. In my case I sense and hear these messages.

As a clairaudient person I can do this. I describe it like tuning in, similar to a radio. I am able to tune- in on a frequency that comes from Archangels and other high beings. I can hear specific messages and can communicate with these Angels and Spirits. I know this may sound kooky to some non-believers of the psychic phenomena, but it's true.

Equal energy exchange was explained to me by these higher spirits of knowledge as I wrote in the previous pages. They told me that humans have not been "asking" the correct way to manifest what they want, need or desire. I showed you briefly in the 1o things you should know section of the book. But the details are the key to success with manifesting.

We all know there are tons of books that you can read about how to manifest what you want. Not one book explains it with equal energy. These Angel guides laughed about this as I communicated with them. They said to me: *"Wow, we made things so simple. You and your human friends constantly make life on earth dimension difficult for themselves. Don't they know we are here to help them and all they have to do is Ask correctly?"* I agreed. I said back "we humans" do complicate everything. It seems we don't take time to see or feel without being rushed!

164

I like to use the example of how "we humans" work so much, (well, most of us) and we forget to take time for ourselves to Breathe, I mean literally take long deep breaths in and out! It sounds silly, think about the last time you really took a long deep breath in and out. Unless you are a Yogi, most of us don't do this or think about doing it.

I asked the Angels to educate me. They said, *"Yes, and would you please share this information with other humans."* I said yes.

THE TASK

My task is to teach all humans "how to: manifest what you want and desire with equal energy exchange." I am making it simple to manifest, as I was specifically advised by the higher educated beings and Angels. Basically, all those energies of the light (positive energy) that want "us humans" to succeed and be happier in our lives on earth.

The guides joke a lot with me when they said: *"humans chose to make life difficult. Life was simple until humans made it complicated. Humans create their own chaos."*
  Maybe they weren't joking. I guess it's up to us "humans" to figure out what we want and need, then manifest it!

On the next pages, I wrote how to specifically "manifest." You can follow the guidelines and of course you can add what you like or take out some things to your preference. But, "Please remember the most important part **DO NOT** take out- the equal exchange!" That was a message I just heard from the Angels. They made me write that bold and big in the book.

Oh, the Angels just told me that some of you reading this book are saying in your heads "who am I to ask such high spirits like Angels or God to help me?"

This is the Angels answer (I heard it loud and clear*)" We allow you to ask for what you want. It is not being selfish. Only when you ask without the equal exchange you will feel selfish."* *"Understand that all people deserve good things in life. That includes you!" The purpose for all of life to use this equal energy exchange is to balance the worlds, earth and beyond. All humans affect each other. All humans affect the earth. All of earth affects our universes."*

That was clear enough for me. The Angels also want to express the following directions when you start to manifest: *"Make sure when you take the moment to ask us for what it is you need, that you are specific as possible. WE get a lot of requests here and we need to help you the best we can, be specific on all asking, give us "your time-moment and location" by stating a month and year also a place. We want to bring what is needed. "*There is no "time" where they are. The Angels explained to me they use the term moment. We humans invented the clock.

They said they can get as close as they can , to our "time" as to their "moment" to bring us opportunities and what we are asking to come into our lives on earth.

"There is much importance in you stating your true desire, you intention, and knowing you deserve what you are asking for. Remember, every thought you have during, before and after "asking" is energy, so make the human thought of what it "is"- to be positive."

Okay I'm butting in for a bit. The Angels are trying to explain that everything we say, meaning if it is our voice or our thought in our head, is energy.

When doing your manifesting, if you say in your head or aloud, what you wanted and afterwards you think or you use the expression "if it's meant to be -it will happen, or maybe it will

166

come true." That is a big a no, no! You then instantly negated what you asked for by 1) Not believing it would happen, 2) placing uncertain energy which is negative or null. That means you just wasted your time! The manifest message was distorted and won't get to them!

POSITIVE PLEASE
The idea is to be positive. Use only positive words and make sure you intend on receiving what you are asking. Because you deserve good things in your life! I want to clarify; I do suggest manifesting good tangible things in life but also good people or relationships. You will know what I mean by the outlined, very detailed examples. I made these tailored for you to follow. I actually wrote each of them so there's no way you will self-sabotage it. My wording is mint, straight from Archangel Michael!

Okay let the manifesting begin.
 Wait one more thing, the Angels just spoke to me and said, *and "Tell humans to only repeat their manifest once a week-their time! Otherwise, they will just be saying words without truly "feeling it, the desire of it will be lost, if they over ask- and the intent will be gone." Manifest* once a week only, please.
 Sometimes I think the Angels may be saying that because they do get a humongous amount of requests and hearing them over and over must drive them crazy! Just kidding, that was just a "thought" of humor.

Seriously, if you say something over and over, it is just words that don't mean Shizzle. If you are taking the time and effort, do it all the way-correctly!

MANIFEST

Go for it:
First make a list of everything you desire in life. It can be a

loving relationship, happiness, better job or new one, a puppy or money to pay the bills. Make a list of what you want or need. This will help you find your "voids" in life. Then you can best manifest to fill the voids with positive people, things or thoughts.

* note I want to explain that we all look at situations in a different way than others. If you use the word "happy" to describe something or someone, happy *to you* can have a different meaning than "happy" to me. This is most likely due to how we were taught.

Be specific, if you use the word "happy, "make it detailed for example "happy emotionally" or happy because they are secure in their life, this can mean monetarily or of sound minded. Be specific!

Below are examples for you to follow and understand the equal energy exchange way of asking.

1) Manifesting a "Good Match," relationship.
YES, how did you guess? This *is* the most popular!
2) Manifesting a job
3) Manifesting stuff (tangible items)
4) Manifesting knowledge & receiving self-realization- (this can also be used to manifest how to change your thought process to be more positive.)
5) Manifesting Money $

MANIFESTING A "GOOD MATCH"

Take 3 long breaths in and 3 exhales out at your own pace. Sit in a place you feel comfortable and peaceful, indoors or outdoors. Try to *feel* in your heart. Focus by holding your chest area with your hands then know your body and mind are connected. You can state this aloud or within.

Continue with your focus on "Asking equally" to manifest your Match.

I am and I allow myself to meet a _____ (say man or woman, you don't need a name)
that has healthy habits, that is respectful to me and I to them. They are attracted to me sexually, intellectually, physically and emotionally and I to them. We love each other 100%; we are monogamous to each other (if that's what you want). We communicate properly and nicely to each other, we understand to each other's feelings and way of thinking. We are happy together and trust each other. We are each other's good match and we deserve each other. We meet __month and year __ (insert a month and year you wish) earth dimension.

Options to insert if you choose, you may also add what *you* desire of your "good match."
They have a good paying job
They are humorous
You are both available to meet each other
They have values similar to yours or values you admire
You accept each other's "normals"
They are specifically good looking example: tall, physically fit, blue eyes yada yada...
They are Abundant in money
They are psychically healthy, emotionally sound.
They are human (I'm just being funny- I hope this is a given LOL)

> A Note- Remember, the Angels said, "You can't be someone's "good match, if you aren't theirs. This is equal energy exchange."

MANIFESTING A JOB

Take 3 long breaths in and 3 exhales out at your own pace. Sit in a place you feel comfortable and peaceful, indoors or outdoors. Try to *feel* in your heart, focus by holding your chest area with your hands then know your body and mind are connected. You can state this aloud or within.

Continue with your focus on asking equally for your new opportunity.

I am and I allow myself to get hired at (plug in the name of the employer or type of job you desire here.) I will receive a fair contract. Both of us (employer/person) will be happy with the contract. I will honestly do the best job I can. I will be best employee I can for (put company/employer). In return, the company pays me in (put you amount you want fair and reasonable) amount of US dollars or more.

We (you and employer) are both happy and satisfied with the work I contribute. I am positive for the (company name or employer), myself and all of the companies customers (if any, depending on job)

I receive this job (plug in date and year) November 2016 (insert a month and year) earth dimension. We both help each other and respect each other in all aspect of business and work ethics. We have an equal energy exchange.

This asking for a job can be done very specific if needed. Write in a company's name you with to work for, or bosses name to hire you.

If you have a specific field you are looking for you can word it towards that occupation.

If you want a job in another location, meaning another office, town, state, country, please fill that information in the appropriate area.

I feel you get the jest of this one!

MANIFESTING STUFF

Take 3 long breaths in and 3 long exhales out at your own pace. Sit in a place you feel comfortable and peaceful, indoors or outdoors.

Try to *feel* in your heart, focus by holding your chest area with your hands then know your body and mind are connected. You can state this aloud or within.

Continue with your focus on asking equally your desired items.

I am and I allow myself to receive a <u>Bike</u> (add what you desire here). I will do my very best to take care of this bike the best I can, I will also exercise with it, appreciate it, and if needed lend it to a friend. For receiving this bike I will be grateful that I have the strength and opportunity to find, purchase or receive it and will express my gratitude appropriately. I deserve a bike. I will use it properly and be careful of others while I ride it. I receive this bike August 2014(add you date here) earth dimension.

Depending on what you are asking for you can make it equal in some way. You can see how inventive you can be when you desire something badly. Your wording will change due to the item you are asking to come to you. It is okay just keep the exchange positive.

Some people have been gifted, won or "found monies" to receive what they were asking appropriately for, that was how the items came to them.

MANIFESTING KNOWLEDGE & SELF-REALIZATION

Take 3 long breaths in and 3 exhales out at your own pace. Sit in a place you feel comfortable and peaceful, indoors or outdoors. Try to *feel* with your heart, focus by holding your chest area with your hands then know your body and mind are connected. You can state this aloud or within.
 Continue with your focus on asking equally for knowledge & self-realization.

 I am and I allow myself to understand my mind and body. I would like to ask my higher self the all-knowing me- my soul to help me receive clarity and truly understand to collect knowledge of my human self (put here what you want information, clarity or knowledge of) With this information, I will have self-realization of what I need to know in this lifetime to advance myself in all aspects of my life this year of _____ through the rest of my life!(or a specific one, for example doing better at school or letting go of old negative relationships , prejudices, selfishness or being a victim of others taking advantage of your "niceness"). This knowledge I will be a better person.

 I will have self-love and I can treat others better when I understand myself. I can teach others about my experiences and how they might relate to them. I   want to have self-understanding as well as understanding others; I will look through other people's eyes or situations. I will also understand myself. I want to know more about my body and mind. I want and deserve to live happier. My knowledge is freedom; I can have it and share it with others. I receive this knowledge and self-realization *add month and year here* earth dimension.

You may have something that happened to you in your lifetime that you want clarity about, this would be something you would plug in and ask about specifically.

*"Humans sometimes hear us but they need to **realize** and **accept** the information."*

MANIFESTING MONEY

Take 3 long breaths in and 3 long exhales out at your own pace. Sit in a place you feel comfortable and peaceful, indoors or outdoors.

Try to *feel* in your heart, focus by holding your chest area with your hands then know your body and mind are connected. You can state this aloud or within.

Continue with your focus on asking equally for manifesting money and abundance. Trust that money will come your way.

I am and I allow myself to create from me (these are options you can choose one or all) working for it, or by receiving or finding or winning large amounts of money of (Put a desired amount) _ or more. With this money I will take care of my responsibilities, I will live within my means. I will share and help others if needed. I do this without wanting anything in return except a thank you (you must mean this part!) I can and I will bring money and abundance of opportunities to myself. I deserve this money to better my life and my family's life. What energy I give out, I will receive without expecting. What is deserved will come my way December 2016(place your date here) earth dimension.

Other options and phrases you can add for manifesting money and abundance:

What I strive for will bring money my way from my work efforts.

Money can be new way of work or salary.

It could be wining an item and selling it for money.

I am open to receive money or values from the positive ways.

I will treat others as I like to be treated and all abundance I am responsible for in positive way.

BE WELL, MANIFEST EQUAL ENERGY-ALWAYS

The universes work in many ways, if you keep it positive, the return will be abundant whether it is money or lots of love.
The Angels want to share this last message to you all.

"Positive always breeds positive."
Be well, enjoy your new life of equal energy exchange and know you deserve goodness in your lives- share this knowledge with others.

"Every exchange is important; it reflects on the worlds- yours, ours, all energies of existence ... we are all souls that live together."

The psychic teacher signed the email that was attached to the book download with the word Gratitude and wrote:

I appreciate that you took the time to read this book, please give it to another person for a positive energy exchange!

That is the end of the book from the psychic teacher. It was interesting because it was a bit of this and that, all mixed in, but good info.

Back to Sonny and Cher

After they read the book; they sat and performed the soul talk that their psychic teacher suggested for them. It was written step by step in the book previously inserted. That next morning, Cher texted Sonny wanting to talk about all of what she felt from the soul talk meditation- They met at the Duncan Doughnuts at 10am. They picked the one that was closest to Sonny's apartment.

Sonny and Cher claimed they both felt a feeling of release and

174

revitalization. Sonny said she felt shame lifted from her body in a euphoric way. Cher explained the feeling as a loving movement of warm energy that swept over her. It was good to know they learned a lesson. It was super great to know they felt better and were putting an end to their ignorant behaviors.

Next Thursday Dinner Number six

The ladies walked into the restaurant for the last dinner to review the foods consistency for Sonny's Frommez writing assignment. They sat down in the same table as their five previous dinners. They were feeling great since their auras were clean and balanced. Cher just had hung her purse on the back of her chair and Dev walked over to them and said:

Dev: Hi Lori and Dee!
Nice to have you back again. I was really hoping you would come in tonight. I have something special for you.

Dee aka Sonny: Hi... Oh really, that sounds great but we are going to get the same dish we always get.

Dev: Oh no. I didn't mean a Special on the menu- wait- I'll be right back.

Lori aka Cher: What is he talking about?

Dee aka Sonny: Who knows... he's just cute no matter what he says!

Dev: Look, Dee- you know how we have 41 pasta dishes here on the menu.

Dee & Lori: Yes.

Dev: Okay here's a menu and look we added one more.

Lori: Look its number 42 called DEE Lori's number 42- it's our concoction- and our recipe!

175

Dev: Yep.

The owner is actually my cousin, he really was into your special order and thought since you two were nice ladies and regulars that he wanted to add it- he was reprinting the menus. Now you are famous. My cousin, his name is Drew. He wants to say hello, but he's also the chef. He said maybe after your done eating he can talk to you? If, you don't mind…

Lori: OMG that's so cool- tell him thank you. This is amazing!

Dee: I know! An epic moment! - I am totally going to tell everyone to come here! Literally!
Great we can't wait to meet him.
Dev: Okay let me put your orders in and I'll bring it out shortly.

Lori: How about that. We have food named after us! I'm TWEETING it right now!
Dee: I know! *How* cool is that! We *are* special!

Lori: Did *you* mind control him into doing that?
Dee: Not without permission…Hahahha!

Sonny and Cher – I meant, Dee and Lori- ate their dinners and were really stoked. It was an impressive restaurant, although it was a casual eating place- it had great food and it was consistently "on point" according to Dee and Lori.

Dev: Are you done eating?
Dee and Lori: Yes. Thank you.

Dev: My cousin can come say hello now; I'll tell him your done eating okay... Be back in a sec.

Dee: I am going to ask Dev how old he is.
Lori: What! Why?

Dee: Because you like him. And I am.
Lori: Please don't.
Dee: But this is our last supper- no pun intended.
Lori: Shut it- here they come…

Dev: This is my cousin Drew.
Drew: Hi ladies- you must be Lori and Dee. I really loved the ingredients you put together, ya know the dish you created- I tried it last week after seeing it over and over. I figured it must be tasty. I ate it for dinner last night. The fried egg was surprisingly a good addition to the dish and complimented the other ingredients nicely. That's when I noticed *you*- a few weeks ago when you first came in the restaurant.

Lori: Oh thank you… it was just. I don't know- something that sounded good together.
Dee: Thank you, for crediting us on the menu- that was quite an honor and surprise! Thanks.

Drew: No problem. Hey, Dee- may I ask if you are single?
Dee: Ahhh, yes. I'm, single.

Dee a.k.a. Cher- immediately imagined that T-shirt of the 5 worse things to ask when you meet someone…as Drew asked her "are you single?" Somehow she decided to overlook the blatant pick up line.
Drew continued his conversation with Dee:

Drew: Would you like to go out sometime-? Like to dinner- somewhere else of course- not here..?
Dee: Ahh, sure.
Drew: Cool. Can I call you later? I close the restaurant at 10pm.
Dee: Sure.
Drew: Are you sure that's not too late to call?

Dee: No. No I stay up late, its fine.
Drew: Okay- great. I'll call you later. Excuse me; I have to get back in the kitchen. Nice to meet you -Lori and Dee.

Drew went back to the kitchen to work- it was a busy night at the restaurant. He was slinging pasta all night.
Dev the waiter stood by the table after his cousin walked back to the kitchen and continued to talk to Lori:

Dev: Lori
Lori: Yes.

Dev: Would you like to hang out or something?
Lori: Sure.

Dev: Maybe we can get coffee or something after I'm done work one night? Or tonight- if you want?
Lori: That be awesome- but I like tea.
Dev: Tea it is- can I get your digits?
Lori: Sure.
Dev: Cool.

The ladies paid the check, exchanged numbers with the men and went home happier than the last six weeks as far as I know!

Dee and Lori looked at each other when walking out of the restaurant and said: "I think we are done with the coffee dates."
They were laughing as they walked to their cars.
 Lori and Dee couldn't believe *both* men were *hot* and asked them out.

The following day Lori went out with Dev the waiter -who was also part owner of the restaurant with his cousin. Dev was 26 years old. He was certainly older than he appeared.

 Dee met up with Drew the restaurateur who was 31 years old- they met for lunch and Dee told him that she worked for

Frommerz and had been doing a food consistency review on his restaurant for the last 6 weeks- she mentioned he got 5 stars!

By the way- the restaurant's name was "Twenty Bucks."

Both ladies realized that they manifested a man with all the qualities they asked for! *And* -they did it with respect. They learned the equal energy came to them as the psychic teacher taught them.

That bet the girls had for $60 on who would meet their good match first- well, that was thrown out. Since it was a tie- they met their matches the same night at their final dinner. All was good.

I know you want to know -why did the two ladies use the names Sonny and Cher?
Well, let's say it was some kind of karmic energy of a *couple* - that could bring everything together in harmony. Cheesy. Yes. I know it.

A few days later…

Dee and Lori called the psychic teacher and let her know what happened. They shared that their manifesting came to fruition. They called and left messages for her. They wanted to thank her for changing their energy to be positive and said that they *allowed* themselves to have a new life. They were getting fulfilled. They received a phone call back from the teacher a few days later.

Awakening

During this time the two young ladies confided in me .I heard them clearly- their personalities were alive. Something sparked and *woke me up*.

This is when everything changed for all of us.

Last week when you called me back- you stated you will sign me on. You said that you would represent me as my literary agent.

You sent me the contract of sale for this book along with a great chance of selling it for movie rights. The one you talked about- he was a well-known producer in California.
You were open to reading this book, even though it was written in a unique format of writing. I deeply appreciate that. All of the manifesting from the 2 ladies and me has come true. I believe we are all one.
You had asked me when we spoke the other day in your office "how did all this come about?" You wanted to know what the whole premise behind this fictional story is. Is it real bits and pieces of truth?"

I couldn't answer all of what I wanted- I was pretty nervous and excited at the same time. I wanted to answer you better than I did at that time. I remember my reply was close to this –"I wanted to let you know it was a bit out of my control. The universe wanted me to write. Well, specifically my grandfather. He wanted me to write. He has been deceased for over 20 years now and he came to "visit" me.

Here is what I wanted to expand on- about how and why I wrote the book in this unique way…

One night about a year ago, I was sleeping in bed. I heard a loud rustling of my sliding door. It was the window shades that covered my slider doors in my home. The noise woke me and I saw the clock it was 3:33 am. I assumed it would be my dogs- making the noise. I have two little poodle mixes. They both were sleeping on the bed in my main bedroom. I walked over to the shades to see if they were really moving or if it was my imagination. The shades were definitely moving! There was no draft- no air conditioning blowing on them.
Then, I smelled smoke. No-one   in my house smokes anything. I

checked the stove, the oven… nothing was making the smell. I sniffed around and was wondering why my dogs aren't up helping me.

Then I heard a voice clairaudiently say "hey- "write this down." I will help you. It's time." I instantly knew it was my Italian grandfather. He smoked a pack of cigarettes a day - when he was alive. Alive on earth -that is.

At that moment the shades stopped moving. I walked quickly to my computer and wrote what I heard for 2 hours.

I went back to sleep and around 5:30 ish in the am -he woke me up again! He wanted me to write more.
  He didn't want me to forget the ending of the story. He wanted to tell me the beginning part - the middle and all of the ending. I got up again and continued writing. He said this book will be "it"- a winner.

He told me "it" would have three names on the book cover: my name and two others.

Another year went by and I hadn't heard from my deceased grandfather. Then just a few weeks ago on January 28th at 3:33 am he visited again. He told me the name of the book was to be *Dee Lori's Table 42*. Ergo the 3 names: Dee, Lori and my name as the writer. Since I like numerology- I checked on why the number 42 was in the title.

I researched about them and found that the number four and two added together were six. A number six represents positive energy. Then, I decided to see what the numbers meant separately .The number two is to relax and all will go smoothly. The number four is reconstructing-letting out and bringing new positive ways and organizing. In the story there was a table for two ladies and their characters created the number 42 dish on the menu. I found that interesting- these little ties of information throughout the storyline my grandpa gave me.

It was a combination of food that was brought together for harmony of taste. It felt like when I was writing – these were just small pieces to a puzzle and I was to organize and put them all together for a harmonic balance. This is similar to most things in life.

On January 18th I heard him –my grandfather said "finish the book- the time *is* now". I agreed. On February 14, 2014 also a Full moon- I opened my computer to continue writing.
In the middle of writing-something made me stop to check my email. Inside my mailbox was an email announcement of a contest for a fiction book. The start date for the entry was February 16th, 2014.

Are these Coincidences?
I believe it was a sign, omen or gift of sorts. I entered the writing contest with a celestial combination of ideas -staying up all night and all morning writing. I wrote what I heard from my infinite energy of my grandfather. The puzzle was complete.

I am the proud writer and the psychic teacher in the story- Dee, Lori and the others were all characters I heard from my Angel above.

Thank you for allowing me to email this entire book to you.
I thank you for signing me- and getting me the contract with HH publishing company.
I am proud to have you as my literary agent.

Gratitude-
I look forward to working together.

Sincerely,
Jolie DeMarco

About The Author

J olie is an advocate of high vibrational living– which means
living happy. Jolie created The Mindful Healing Center called
My Flora Aura. She said she wanted to share all the good things
in life—things she loves that bring high vibes!

She is more than an owner of the crystal shop that holds the most
beautiful energy on earth– but an author, inspirational speaker,
intuitive and a conduit of healing energy.

Jolie always says and I quote her "I am just a pipeline of which
positive energy flows through me into others– from verbal
vibration or high vibrations direct from source– that's whomever
you believe in. I am just a messenger and conduit."
  I think that explains a lot. Jolie expresses "I am grateful to do
so for others."

Among her many talents– Jolie wrote 8 books (all available on
AMAZON)—as she explains –8 more on the way. She has a
Healing Mandala oracle card deck available on i-phone and
android. It gives you accurate messages and can be used for self-
healing and meditations. You can feel the magical energies from
the channeled paintings on the front side of the unique cards.

Additionally – Jolie formed an Academy of Telepathy *and*
Academy of Healing Energy. Both offer online workshops to
increase mindfulness and bring higher consciousness while
strengthening your brain functions. You can check it out.
www.AcademyofTelepathy.com

In 2014 Jolie created a young adult and teen mentorship program called YAE Young Adult Empowerment with PREHab4TEENs.com— the concept -helping teens and young adults make the correct choices before they take a wrong path. Jolie loves working people that need guidance. She gives them positive perspectives, helps them advance in life and to make decisions that are mindful. She calls the workshop *mindful messages and mentorship.*

You can follow Jolie DeMarco on YOU TUBE, Facebook and in magazines. Try her workshops – online classes or her website and receive a remote distant psychic reading. www.JolieDeMarco.com

Jolie says she is trying to reach as many people as she can to help them heal with knowledge and happiness. Help her spread the positive energy- Like her on Facebook and share the messages!

Something Free and fun:

Want to see How Intuitive you are? Take a FREE 1 minute test
www.GetaReadingNow.com

My Love and Gratitude

To George DeMarco my grandfather who gifted me messages to write and express. Also to my family, friends and My Flora Aura peeps! Thank you all of you readers- I sincerely appreciate all of you.

Parallel Minds- Jolie DeMarco

Positive Affirmations

Just take 5 minutes a day focus with your intention –what you desire and project. Then state these positive affirmations for balancing your emotions.

I am Love and I am surrounded by Love

I am smart
I am Happy
I Love Life

My Body is Strong
My Mind is awake and alert

I make rational decisions

I fulfill my commitments 100% in a positive way

I am healthy and I have healthy habits

I find solutions without stress

I treat others well- and they treat me well

I enjoy the moments that bring me joy
I am beautiful inside and out

I always do the best I can at everything I do.

I enjoy time for myself- it makes me balanced.

www.ingramcontent.com/pod-product-compliance
Lightning Source LLC
Chambersburg PA
CBHW061208170626
46809CB00003B/1282